HUNTED!

Kit dove for cover. At the same time a chorus of war whoops exploded from the throats of two dozen Blackfoot warriors. Half their number spurred their horses and took off down the trail after Petey. The rest reined off the trail and charged into the undergrowth.

In the scramble, Kit lost track of Gray Feather, and Petey had been too far away to know where he had gotten off to, anyway. Kit could only hope that the coot had hit the ground and found a hole to crawl into. Kit elbowed behind a boulder where the brush grew thicker, backed in among a bramble of raspberries, and drew a pistol.

The crashing of hooves sounded all around him as horses plunged past. Kit waited, listening, hardly breathing. Now there was a different sound. Some of the Indians had dismounted and were beating the brush for him. The snap of a branch riveted his attention. Someone was just on the other side of the boulder. . . .

Other books in the *Kit Carson* series:

#1: THE COLONEL'S DAUGHTER
#2: GHOSTS OF LODORE
#3: REDCOAT RENEGADES
#4: KEELBOAT CARNAGE
#5: COMANCHE RECKONING

KIT CARSON

BLOOD RENDEZVOUS

DOUG HAWKINS

LEISURE BOOKS NEW YORK CITY

For Dick, Mary, Rachel, Alicia, and Drew

A LEISURE BOOK®

March 1999

Published by

Dorchester Publishing Co., Inc.
276 Fifth Avenue
New York, NY 10001

ISBN 0-8439-4499-4

Printed in the United States of America.

ACKNOWLEDGMENTS

My sincerest thanks to the late Dr. Thomas Edward, who so graciously allowed me to roam freely through his rare and valuable collection of monographs by that nineteenth-century Native American scholar, Professor W. G. F. Smith.

BLOOD RENDEZVOUS

Chapter One

The wind sighed through the valley, rippling the stiff brown grass, still carrying with it the faint bite of winter just past. It was a reminiscent chill, one that made Kit Carson recall the long season of popping trees, of frigid nights and cold days, of wading hip deep through icy waters, of setting iron traps, of smearing the bait sticks with castoreum, then returning hours or sometimes days later to retrieve the beaver that the strong scent had lured to the traps hidden beneath the water. If the streams were productive, nearly half the traps might hold a beaver. If they were not, the company would move on to better grounds.

But this trapping season was mostly past. It was spring, time to move down out of the high mountains. Rendezvous was only a few weeks away and already, Kit knew, trappers would be flowing from the hundreds of secluded mountain valleys, streaming to the mouth of Horse Creek—to the site of this year's meeting.

Kit pointed his horse at a nearby ridge and urged it into an easy gait. The company of men behind him, working alongside the river that the trappers called the Gallatin, grew smaller as Kit rode away.

Life for the Rocky Mountain trapper followed the seasons. There was the fall trapping season and then the spring trapping season, when the pelts were at their prime. And in between the men would go into winter quarters, sometimes near a conveniently located fort, like Fort Hall, or just as often, they would move in with a tribe of peaceful Indians. The Nez Percé, Flatheads, or Pend d'Oreilles were usually agreeable winter companions.

But the high point of a trapper's year was the time of the rendezvous, an event held in midsummer when the men made their way out of the mountains, hauling their plews and bear skins, the hard-earned products of their labor, and came together at the great yearly gathering. Eastern merchants and company owners brought gold to pay for the hides, gold that was promptly traded back for whiskey and supplies.

Any gold left over might be spent on the gaudy foofaraws that added status to Indian women's lives, and endeared the women to the white trappers. Everyone was happy. If any coins remained in the bottom of a trapper's hunting bag, they usually disappeared after a couple of hands of Old Sledge. Few men ever left the rendezvous with money in their pockets. What would be the point? There was no place to spend gold in the mountains. But powder and lead, beads and ribbons, tobacco and traps, these were the breath and blood of a mountain man.

Kit wasn't really thinking about the coming rendezvous as his horse pounded the stiff prairie grass and the land climbed beneath its hooves. Below the top of the ridge he reined to a stop and swung out of the saddle. It had been years since he had skylined himself, and he was particularly careful not to do so now. Leaving the horse, Kit covered the last few dozen feet to the ridge in a crouch, easing up to its crest. The snout of his badger-skin hat with its empty staring eye socket, grinning teeth, and the dangling forelegs poked above the ridgeline first. Kit squinted hard against the morning sun, his sharp, blue eyes shifting slowly across the open landscape beyond.

Far to the north the valley shouldered up against pine-covered slopes that swung east and disappeared in the purple haze of vast distances. To the west and south of him rose the dark bulk of the Rocky Mountains. From out of them issued the Gallatin River, its sparkling ribbon of water flowing near where the company of trappers were presently busy with shovels and picks, breaking open the spring sod. Kit's view shifted back to the north and lingered at the base of the trees where long shadows still stretched out, waiting for the morning sun to climb higher in the sky and nibble away at them.

The hairs at the nape of his neck tingled.

They were out there somewhere. The Indians were out there. On and off for the last three days he had seen them, always far off but always there. He'd never gotten close enough to count their numbers, but Kit estimated the size of the party to be around forty strong. It was Blackfoot country, and spying a party of the Indians was nothing unusual. It was the way this particular party kept appearing and disappearing that was odd. Kit wondered if the

Blackfeet were tailing them, or if both parties of men just happened to be traveling in the same direction.

Kit found it incredible that they would not be aware of the trappers' presence. But if they had been, they had made no effort to approach them. Just the same, like a shadow, they were always there—distant, but there.

Kit heard hoofbeats behind him. Gray Feather drew rein and, leaving his pony down by Kit's, hurried up the ridge on foot, then dropped and elbowed up alongside Kit.

"We found the cache. They're all there, just like we left them." Gray Feather inclined his head toward the broad valley that lay before them. "Any sign of the Blackfeet?" Gray Feather was half Ute Indian and half white. His father had insisted on calling him Waldo; his mother had been inclined to give him a *proper* Indian name. The end result was Waldo Gray Feather Smith, as unlikely a combination as one might imagine. The trappers, being a pragmatic lot, simply shortened it to Gray Feather. It was a name that belied the man's extensive education at Harvard College, or the cultured upbringing he had received under his father's charge.

"Not yet," Kit replied, glancing back at the men down by the river. They had uncovered the pit, leaving a pile of sod nearby. One of the men, Maximilian Overmier, was inside it, handing up the bundles of beaver skins that the trappers had hidden there last fall, before moving west and into winter quarters near Fort Hall.

"Do you think they're still out there?"

Kit returned his view to the valley floor. "I don't see 'em, but my neck hairs tell me thar not far off."

"It's unlikely they'll try anything, not with there being thirty-two of us."

"No, they won't try our strength right yet," Kit allowed thoughtfully. "But once we split up we might have us a tussle. We'll have to keep the eyes in the back of our heads wide open. I'll be right pleased when we join up with Bridger and the others at Horse Creek." Kit looked over and grinned. "This child is gonna kick up his heels and have himself a real good time at rend'vou' this year."

Gray Feather shook his head and merely smiled.

"What?" Kit asked when he saw the Indian's disapproval.

"I'll never understand you, or most of the others. You work like jackasses all year, risking life and limb for a handful of gold that you promptly spend."

"Whal, I reckon we all aren't as frugal as you, my friend."

"I like to think that I'm planning for my future, Kit," Gray Feather replied, patting the poke of coins he kept tied securely to his belt in a stout leather pouch.

Kit frowned, but his words were good-natured when he spoke. "Whal, some of us can get by with the company of books and such, and some of us require entertainment of a mite more lusty nature."

"Fighting, dancing, drinking, and card playing have never much interested me."

"I've seen you throw a fist a time or two, pard. And you do shine when you get your dander up."

"Perhaps, but it is not my first choice of entertainment."

Kit laughed. Movement by the river down below caught his eye. Antoine Menard was standing a little way apart from the other trappers, waving an arm at Kit. "Looks like they're calling us back for a powwow."

Kit and Gray Feather scurried down off the ridge and rode back to the waiting party of trappers. As Kit swung off his horse, Jim Huntington, a big, barrel-chested man with a great black beard that climbed up his ruddy cheeks nearly to his dark eyes, stepped away from the cache pit where four bundles of beaver pelts lay upon the winter grass.

"Spy any of them varmints, Kit?" Huntington's deep voice rumbled as he strode forward, one of Sam Hawken's full-stocked rifles swinging in his meaty fist at his side. Where Huntington's moccasins crushed the brittle turf, they left a faint hint of green in their wake from new, spring grass beginning to show.

"Nary a single one, Jim," Kit said, settling his own long rifle easily into the crook of his arm. It was a J. J. Henry fashioned after the Lancaster pattern, stocked to the muzzle with good, straight walnut, mounted in iron, and fitted with a single trigger. It carried thirty-two balls to the pound, as did Huntington's Hawken. Although not nearly as pricy a firearm as the Hawken, Kit's Henry shot true to the mark. There was not a trapper in the party who'd shoot against Kit in a contest, unless they'd had a mite too much Taos Lightning to drink. Not only was Kit the undisputed marksman there, he was also the lead tracker, and as such spent most of his time miles ahead of the main party when they were on the move.

"But they're still out thar, Jim."

Huntington nodded. "If you say so, I'll believe it."

"How did the pelts winter over?"

"Just as we left them in November."

As they talked the two men strode over to the hole that had been cut into the ground last year with extreme care. Putting in a cache had become something of an art to the mountaineers. Roving bands of Indians were always on the lookout for the cache pits of mountain trappers. It was an easy way to hunt beaver, and every tribe knew that a bundle of prime plews could buy more luxuries than they could have ever dreamed of even twenty years earlier.

In putting in a cache of beaver, the sod was carefully cut into blocks and set aside. A hole was dug large enough for a man to work in, and as it went deeper it widened out at the bottom. The trappers were careful to leave no trace of their work and took great pains to haul the dirt far away from the hole on blankets. Rivers were always convenient places to dispose of the excess dirt. Once the hole was finished, it was lined with branches and sticks, and then the bundles of plews carefully set inside, packed tight to the walls of the pit to prevent cave-ins. Finally a blanket or tarpaulin would cover the skins, the hole would be topped with a foot or two of dirt, and the sod carefully placed back over it. Usually trappers remained a day or two on the spot, sometimes picketing their horses over the place to further hide it from detection. If the job had been done correctly, the pelts would be there waiting when the trappers returned for them.

Not only beaver was cached, but oftentimes gunpowder, trade goods, and even firearms were hidden in such a fashion.

A Delaware Indian by the name of Manhead, a full partner in the company, came over. Manhead was dressed in greasy buckskins and smelled of wood smoke and castoreum. Only his high cheekbones and coal-black hair, worn in twin braids below his shoulders, distinguished him from the other white trappers in the company. His buckskin shirt was plain, with none of the beadwork or fancy stitchery that many of the married trappers wore. Upon his head sat a battered, black beaver-felt hat, and a powder horn and hunting bag hung beneath his left arm near the big butcher knife in his belt. In his fist he carried a Lancaster rifle similar to Kit's, only much newer.

Manhead jabbed a thumb over his shoulder toward the men lifting a bale of plews onto one of the packhorses and said, "We did too good a job hiding them. Almost lost this one."

The hillside they were standing upon was peppered with the holes that the men had dug while searching for the exact spot where this cache had been hidden. The pocked landscape looked to Kit like it had taken a blast from a giant shotgun.

Huntington said, "I'd have gophered this whole riverbank if I had to. I'll not leave three hundred pounds of beaver to rot away, no sir."

Manhead glanced at Kit. "Are those Blackfeet still shadowing us?"

"Didn't see them this time, but I'll be sleeping with a pistol in my hand just the same."

The Delaware shook his head. "It is not likely they are there by accident."

"It's no accident," Huntington agreed. "They're staking us out, all right. Eyeing our scalps, I'll wager. And those pack animals too. We're hauling enough beaver to make some buck big medicine in the eyes of his village if he were to bring it in."

Kit said, "The Blackfeet don't worry me so long as I can see the critters. It's when I can't that I start watching my scalp real close. Huntington's right. The Blackfeet know we're gathering in our season's take, and they got thar eyes on it. But up until now we've been too many for them to risk an open attack."

"Which brings us to our next move," Manhead said.

Kit pulled thoughtfully at his chin, feeling the new growth of whisker, hearing them rustle beneath his hand. Kit was one of the few men who shaved on a regular basis—regular being once every other week or so. So far it was going on week two since his cheeks had felt the tug of his razor.

"Unless you boys are willing to spend another month at it, I don't see as we have much choice. Thar's a cache on the Yellowstone, and one on the Jefferson. We can all go together, or we can split up and meet again south of here by the spouting fountains."

Huntington said, "I don't wish to spend any more time than I have to. I've been too long from a jug of sweet sipping whiskey and the arms of the fairer sex. Rocky Mountain boys are more 'an equal to any two or three Blackfeet warriors. I'll take some of the men and head west to the Jefferson. You take the rest with you, Kit. The Yellowstone ain't but an easy two-day ride east."

Huntington's plan was a practical solution to their problem. They had two caches to recover, in two opposite directions, and enough men between them to make any band of hostile Indians think twice about causing trouble. Just the same, Kit was uneasy with the offhanded manner that Huntington dismissed the Blackfoot threat.

"I'll go east," Kit agreed. "We'll divide the men between us, but you take the greater portion and the plews with you. I'll take Manhead with me, because he has a nose for finding the caches." Kit had not been with the company when the Yellowstone cache had been buried. At that time last December and January, Kit had been in Taos, attending his friend Charles Bent's wedding. "Once we dig it up we'll work our way up the Yellowstone to the spouting fountain and wait for you and your boys. We'll take our time, set a few traps along the way. That should give you enough time to make it back. The Jefferson is a sight farther off than the Yellowstone."

"I hear the beaver do shine on the Yellowstone this time of year," Huntington said with a grin. "You'll pick up some fine pelts before they start to grow their summer coats."

"Maybe. Just don't go and get yourself scalped, Huntington. Blackfeet are some when it comes to scalpin'. And I promised Old Gabe we'd all sit down with him and swap tales over roasted hump-ribs and boudins. I wouldn't want to let him down."

Huntington laughed and boasted, "Our Rocky Mountain boys are some too, Kit. Ain't a man among us who hasn't taken a Blackfoot scalp a time or two. We'll be at Horse Creek to share victuals with Bridger just like you promised him. Just make sure you keep an eye on your back trail. Wouldn't want no black-eyed savage lifting that pretty thatch of yeller hair of yours now."

By this time the men had three bundles of beaver pelts tied onto the pack frames. Overmier was throwing a loop over a fourth pack and cinching it down tight. Menard and another Delaware named Owl Man, Manhead's cousin, were riding toward the ridge, presumably to see for themselves if the Blackfeet had really vanished. Gray Feather and Joe Meek stood down by the river, talking. Joe was pointing to the south where the Gallatin issued from the mountains, and Gray Feather was nodding his head. All around the gently sloping hillside trappers were sprawled upon the ground, taking in the pleasant spring sun, swapping tales, chewing jerked venison, smoking what tobacco they had left. It had been a long winter, and everyone was looking forward to the coming rendezvous.

Owl Man and Menard returned to report they had seen no Blackfeet in the vicinity. Kit and Huntington divided the company between them. The packhorses would go with Huntington, and he would take extra men to handle them and protect them if the need should arise. Kit picked six men for the quick trip to the Yellowstone, while Huntington took the other twenty-five with him.

With the sun standing straight overhead, the men saddled up and broke into two companies. Manhead and his cousin said good-bye to each other. Kit drew up alongside Huntington's mount. "I'll be looking for you in about two weeks."

"We'll be coming back by way of the Madison River. I'll meet you at the spouting fountain."

The two trappers shook hands and Kit turned his men away, starting east. Huntington's boys left the Gallatin and rode west. They had left the cache pit open. There was no need to hide it now that the precious pelts had been recovered. All up and down the secluded valleys of the Rocky Mountains scores of such holes peppered the landscape, some dozens of years old. The scars of old cache pits might remain on the land for a hundred years or more, Kit reckoned. They were a sure sign to future travelers that white men had been through these distant lands. A true testament to the trappers' tenacious spirit to any who might happen upon them in the future.

Chapter Two

In the two days it took for Kit and his band of trappers to reach the Yellowstone River, they saw neither hide nor hair of a single Blackfoot. Even the hair at the nape of his neck—those telltale harbingers of danger that for Kit were more true than any compass point—were not bristling. Kit was worried about Huntington's group, for the safety of the men and pelts in his charge. Clearly if the Blackfeet were not following Kit, then they must have turned onto Huntington's trail. But Huntington's company was twenty-five men strong, Kit reminded himself. Every one of them was a seasoned mountaineer who knew the way the stick floated when it came to Indians. Kit shoved the concern to the back of his brain, telling himself that in a time of danger, Jim Huntington would know what to do.

Following the lay of the land, Kit had to take the trappers north first, even though the Yellowstone lay due east. They reached the river at a place where it flowed gently through wide plains and pine-covered mesas. They followed it south, as it wound through shallow canyons that grew deeper with the miles. The first night on the river they made camp in a sheltered draw. Although they had seen not a single Indian, Kit set up a rotation of guards just in case.

As the men crowded close to their campfires after eating their evening meal, Kit strolled by himself a little way along the Yellowstone to think. A few minutes later Manhead found Kit along the river smoking his pipe, his buffalo robe wrapped around him to ward off the chill of the late-spring night.

Kit looked up at the crunch of moccasins upon the gravel bank.

"The cache, it is yet several miles south," Manhead told him, knowing that Kit had been in Taos part of the season, attending Charles Bent's wedding to the pretty Spanish senorita, Ignacia Jaramillo, when this particular cache had been made.

"Tomorrow?"

"Yes. Tomorrow we will be there."

"Good. The sooner we get on down south, the better I'll like it."

"You think the Blackfeet are still near?"

In the darkness Kit made a wry smile. "It's not like them to be on thar best behavior when a company of trappers are in thar neighborhood. And I can't believe they don't know we're here."

"Maybe something changed their minds?" Manhead suggested. "Maybe they knew many would die if they attacked us."

"Maybe." But Kit was not convinced. The Indian that made Kit most nervous was the Indian that he didn't see. And Kit was feeling right jittery at the moment. He and the Delaware walked back to the campfires. The trappers had started spreading out their bedrolls and curling up with their rifles. Gray Feather was sitting near one of the fires, leaning toward it so that the flickering yellow light showed upon the pages of the thick book in his hands.

Kit hunkered down beside him. "What are you reading thar? More of them Shakespeare yarns?" Gray Feather had studied English literature while at Harvard College, and the half-breed always had his nose stuck in a book. Books made Kit uneasy. He was suspicious of things he did not understand, reading being one of them. Most men had learned to cipher their letters on their mama's knee when they were but tykes, but growing up on the wild Missouri frontier, Kit had always found many more important things to occupy himself with. Now he wished he had taken the time to learn to read, although he'd not openly admit that to any man—except perhaps to Gray Feather, whom he had come to think of as a brother in spite of the wide differences between them.

"They are plays," Gray Feather said patiently. "Shakespeare wrote plays and sonnets. James Fenimore Cooper writes *yarns*."

"Who?"

"Never mind." Gray Feather closed the thick book upon his finger to mark the place. "I know that look. You're worried about something, Kit. It's those Blackfeet, isn't it?"

"It ain't like 'em just to sashay away, especially after dogging our trail for the last three days." Kit tapped his pipe out upon his palm. "Manhead thinks something might have happened to change thar minds."

"And what do you think?"

Kit shook his head. "I don't know what to think for sure. I'd be right pleased if that was the straight of it, Gray Feather." Kit could see no point in worrying the men with his suspicions that the Blackfeet had turned onto Huntington's trail.

"But you don't think so."

Kit stood. "I'm gonna get some sleep, I've got the third watch." He started toward his bedroll, then turned back. "What I think is you, me, none of us ought to stray too far from our rifles." Kit wheeled back and disappeared into the shadows.

Manhead stood with his back hard against a tall pine tree battered by years of harsh winters and violent summer storms. He pointed his nose at a spire of rock across the river, two hundred yards off. He stood there a moment in narrowed-eyed concentration, adjusted two inches to his left, squinted again, then, taking a measured stride, paced off exactly eleven steps. He stopped and bounced his weight upon the ground, testing it. He moved a step farther and tried it again. Then two steps to the left, and one more time he assayed the earth for a suspicious springiness.

Manhead pointed at his toes. "Dig here."

At once two trappers put shovels to the sod and began clawing large chunks from the ground. The earth was still wet from the spring thaws and it readily yielded to their spades. In a few minutes they hit the top blanket, and soon afterward were lifting packets of beaver pelts from the hole.

It was late afternoon by time they had recovered the valuable skins. Kit decided to remain there for the night, and after giving the orders to the campkeeper to set up, he and Gray Feather mounted their horses and rode down the valley to a place where it widened out. They rode up the rocky slope to a high point of land that offered a view to the northeast.

Reining to a halt at the rim of the valley, Kit

shaded his eyes to the west and made a slow, careful scan of the open country before them.

"Not even a lonely buffalo," Gray Feather noted after both men had sifted the distance for more than ten minutes.

"Makes you wonder, don't it?" Kit mused. "What are they up to?"

"Maybe Manhead was right, Kit. Maybe something changed their minds."

"Hmm, I wonder. What would distract Blackfeet from lifting our scalps?"

Gray Feather shrugged. "Could be a lot of things. This Yellowstone country is also home to the Crows. They might have run into a band of them and are off having themselves a grand old fight—there is no love lost between Crows and Blackfeet, you know." Gray Feather paused and thought a moment. "Or the Blackfeet might have decided to pursue something they valued more than our scalps."

Kit and Gray Feather looked at each other.

"The pelts," they said at the same time, each man finally voicing the concern that had been quietly eating away at them.

Kit rocked back in his saddle, concern cutting deep into his brow. "It's Huntington and the others they're after."

"We don't know that for certain, Kit," Gray Feather said.

Kit thought a moment. "Huntington's got a heap of mountain savvy. He knows what way the stick floats, and he wouldn't let a band of Injuns catch him by surprise." Even as he said it, Kit knew he was only trying to convince himself of the truth of that.

"He's got most of the men along with him, too," Gray Feather added. "The Blackfeet don't like to fight a battle they don't know they can win."

"Can't they? Thar must have been thirty or forty warriors the last I seen them."

"Like you said, Huntington has got mountain savvy."

Kit and Gray Feather turned their horses away from the rimrock and started back to the camp. They had entered prime beaver country, and even though the Yellowstone River had been trapped regularly ever since Francois Larocque of the old North West Company had first smeared castoreum on a bait stick back in 1805, it still managed to produce large catches.

By the time they rode back into camp, the trappers were already out making their sets. The campkeeper had arranged their housekeeping, had a cook fire burning, and was preparing the stretching and drying frames. The company worked together like a finely made and oiled chronometer. Each man had a job to do, and each did it superbly well. In a large brigade such as this one had been before splitting up, jobs were delegated. Some trapped, some skinned, some cooked. Whenever Kit trapped alone, or with only one or two other men, every bit of trapping, skinning, scraping, stretching, and cooking became each man's task. Kit liked the "company" system. Life was much easier in a brigade . . . and a lot safer.

Although the Blackfoot threat was not forgotten, the persistent worry over an attack faded into the background as the small company of mountaineers trapped their way south. Kit moved the men slowly, making camp often and for several days at a time, intending to give Huntington and his men plenty of time to retrieve the last cache and make their way from the Jefferson to the Madison, then up the Madison River to the place where they had planned to meet. As the days passed the land around them climbed and the valley of the Yellowstone River grew narrower and steeper.

Around the campfires in the evenings the men told stories of what lay ahead of them. Some in the company had never been to this place of spouting waters, bubbling mud pits, and steaming, sulfurous lakes as blue as the finest Mexican turquoise and clear as a baby's conscience.

"If you flung a bullet into one of 'em, it would sink clear to the heart of the Earth," Antoine Menard was telling a pair of greenhorns.

"No. Is it true?" This was Carlos Archuleta, a young, stocky Mexican. Archuleta had come out with Kit from Taos that winter. Archuleta looked to Kit Carson now for some sign.

Kit said, "Menard tells it straight, Carlos. We'll be there tomorrow, and you can see for yourself."

Joe Meek had been listening to the talk. He said, "First time I ever lay eyes on the place, I was two steps ahead of a Blackfoot war party. Arras war a-comin' at me from ever' direction, they war. Whal, my mustang come a-riding over this here rise, and when we went plunging down the other side of it we war suddenly swallowed up by this cloud of steam. It war so thick I couldn't see the sun no more, and smelled of brimstone. All of a sudden I thought that one of them arras had done me in and I'd crossed over the river into the hereafter. Only it warn't streets of gold I was seeing, nor any heavenly smells neither. I figured I went to the other place. But when I seen this here feller standin' thar with a long tail and a pitchfork in his hands an' wavin' me home, I knew I'd gone the wrong way. I yanked back on the reins, wheeled my mount head to tail, and vamoosed outta thar. And I ain't never been back since, no sir. I war so thankful to be outta thar that I made me a pack with the Lord never to use his name in vain again. I even went to church last year at rend'vous when Reverend Parker come out with Whitman and done services for the Flatheads thar."

Archuleta's mouth fell open. His wide eyes didn't blink for a long moment. "But what of the Indians that were following you?" he asked finally.

"Oh, them. Whal, lucky for me they seen the apparition too. Why, they turned about faster than a dog chasing his own tail. They skedaddled out of thar so fast, the ground beneath thar horses' hooves went to smokin' worse than ol' Mephistopheles hisself!"

Slowly the trappers began to chuckle. Archuleta glanced at them, grinning sheepishly as he realized he'd been greened by Meek, then he laughed with the rest of them.

Kit said, "Joe had it mostly right, Carlos. 'Cept for that part about the fellow with the pitchfork and tail, I reckon."

"Whal, I could have swore he was a-standin' thar, Kit," Meek retorted, not willing to let a good joke die its natural death.

Two weeks after splitting up from Huntington and his boys, Kit brought his party to a place where the Yellowstone River cut into a deep canyon and plunged down spectacular falls. They had left the riverbanks some hours earlier and now watched the spectacle from a high rimrock overlooking it. As the spray rose in the clear blue sky, a rainbow arched over the falls, each leg of it seemingly resting upon either side of the Grand Canyon of the Yellowstone, as the trappers called it.

"Now, thar's a sight you don't see every day," Kit declared.

"Magnificent!" Gray Feather exclaimed, moving

his horse near the edge of the canyon, a most unusual show of wonderment from a man normally afraid of great heights.

Kit grinned. "You got a poem in mind to describe it?" It was Gray Feather's way to come up with something appropriate to say whenever a thing stirred his soul, as this sight obviously had. Usually it was a quote from some writer whom Kit had never heard of. Like the time they had stood beneath the towering entrance to the canyon of the Green River and Gray Feather had recited a portion of Southey's poem "The Cataract of Lodore."

"I'm speechless, Kit. I can't think of one."

"That must be some kind of a first for you, pard!"

Gray Feather looked over his shoulder at Kit. "But I can probably think of something if you really want me to."

"I prefer to leave things just as they are. I wouldn't want you to go smudging up God's splendid Creation with the simple words that mere mortals can put together."

"Where are all the bubbling brimstone cauldrons?" Archuleta asked.

"Cauldrons?" Menard hooted. "I want to see me one of them men with the tail and pitchfork!"

"Let's see if we can scare us up one," Kit replied, smiling, starting the company toward the southwest. It wasn't long before the land around them began to steam from dozens of vents in the earth. The odor of sulfur filled the air and vaporous wraiths floated past the men as they rode through the strange landscape. Kit led them around a huge pit of bubbling mud to its crusty edge, where they paused to marvel at the sight. Some of the men stuck hands into the pit and declared it nearly hot enough to boil a goose egg.

"Now you boys keep your eyes peeled for that

feller with the pitchfork. He war right around here someplace," Joe Meek warned them sternly. If there was a devil about, Kit figured it was Joe himself, judging by the glint in the young trapper's eye. But Kit *was* keeping his eyes peeled, and he *was* looking for devils—the sort that carried bows and arrows, and scalping knives, and went by the name of Bug's Boys, "Bug" being the mountain man's nickname for "Satan."

Saddling up, the trappers pushed on, passing bubbling pools of thick mud, small, deep blue lakes, and long, snaking cracks in the earth that spit hot water and hissed brimstone and steam. Kit was moving the party to the west where the spouting fountain lay. It was still a full day's ride to where he'd agreed to meet Huntington and his boys, and as the sun lowered ahead of them the men began eyeing the forest for a likely place to set up camp and build a fire out of sight of any passing Blackfeet.

Kit led the way along a game trail down into one of the valleys. Almost at once he become suspicious of the trace they had chosen. For a game trail it appeared remarkably well trodden. Then a hoofprint caught his eye and he reined to a halt, leaping lightly off his horse.

"What's the matter, Kit?" Gray Feather asked as the mountain man hunkered down over the trail. The company remained mounted, waiting for Kit to thoroughly study the signs in the hard ground.

"Horses," Kit said finally. "Three of four of 'em been through here not long ago. Looks like someone's been using this way right regular. Some of these tracks are weeks old, others were made a day or two ago."

"Bug's Boys?" one of the trappers asked in a hushed voice. Every man was suddenly alert, their rifles ready, eyes and ears straining for any hint that their deadly enemy might be near.

"I'd say not," Kit replied. "In fact, I'd say these prints were made by a white man's horses."

"Do you know of any trappers working this stretch of territory, Kit?" Meek asked, his joviality of the last several hours suddenly replaced with a quiet concern.

"I don't know of any, but that doesn't mean thar isn't a party nearby, or even a loner."

"A loner? A man would be a fool to trap Injun country all by hisself, and I know what I'm talking about," Meek exclaimed. "I war trapping the Rocky Fork of the Yellowstone last fall with Bridger before our company split and I joined up with you boys. Went off on my own for a couple days to try some likely beaver water, when the next thing I know, the Crows showed up and took me. I thought I'd gone beaver that time, but I managed to jawbone my way out of that fix . . . until Bridger and about a hunder' of our mountain boys came to treat with them. When it war all over the Crows made a treaty with Blanket Chief—that's what they called Bridger—for three months. They named me *Shiam Shaspusia*, because they said I could outlie the Crows."

Kit said, "Whoever he is, he can't be too far up ahead. I judge these tracks to be his regular coming and going. Let's take a look."

Kit stepped up into his saddle and got his horse moving. Quietly, the men followed behind him single file. The trail wound down toward a stream. The trappers heard the tumbling water long before they saw it. From somewhere below the odor of wood smoke wafted up on the chill evening air. When the trees parted to reveal a small clearing, the men came to a halt. Before them lay the crude makings of a trapper's camp. A single horse picketed there looked over at them. A fire smoldered off to one side with a Dutch oven suspended over it from a tripod. A coffeepot sat upon a bank of coals. Nearby, a lean-to faced the fire pit. Inside the crude shelter was a mat of pine boughs and a few crumpled blankets. Some drying meat hung from a tree limb, and to one side stood two stretching frames, one holding the pelt of a freshly skinned beaver.

The owner of the camp was not around.

"Looks like a loner," Joe Meek said softly as he looked around the campsite.

"From the appearance, I'd say the fellow will be back shortly," Gray Feather noted.

"Reckon we ought to wait for him. It wouldn't be neighborly to not stop and pay a visit." Kit swung a leg over the pommel of his saddle, but before he could light upon the ground a voice called out from the cover of some nearby rocks.

"Set one foot in my camp, hoss, and ye're a dead man. Betsy here has got her eye on ye and she's a-wearing a hair trigger today!"

Chapter Three

Kit stopped in midmotion, then very slowly settled himself back upon the saddle. His sharp eyes probed the rock that concealed the man but saw nothing. "If you're shy of having some company, we'll be on our way," Kit called to the unseen man.

"No, ye won't. Not so fast." This time the voice came from another location. The man had moved. Whoever he was, he was quick on his feet and quiet as a ghost.

Kit shifted his view, but all he could see was the rising rocky ground, mostly overgrown with pine trees. A man could hide real good in that, Kit mused. He'd be hard to uproot, but Kit had no intention of flushing this bird. If he wanted to be left alone, Kit was willing to oblige him. But being left alone did not seem to be what the man had in mind just yet.

"How did ye coons find me?" the voice demanded.

"We weren't looking for you," Kit called back. As he spoke he was aware that the trappers behind him were slowly moving their horses off the trail. If he could keep him talking long enough, one or two of his men might be able to melt into the shadows and come around on the fellow. "We were looking for a place to spend the night—someplace where Blackfeet aren't likely to spot our cook fires."

"Blackfeet? Ye seen them red devils?"

"Seen some a while back. None recent. But this is prime Injun country, friend, and this child don't take chances."

There was a long pause, and when the stranger replied, his voice came from a third direction. "Ye come to steal my plews too, I'll wager! Hah. Well, the joke's on ye, hoss." From his hiding place the man cackled. "Ye went and wasted your time hunting down ol' Petey Pauly, ye did!"

Stealing a glance to his men, Kit saw that Meek and Gray Feather had disappeared into the dense growth crowding the trail they had followed.

"No one here wants to steal your winter's gather, friend. We're passing through. Got to meet our partners ahead."

"Partners? Then there will be more of ye?"

"A few, I reckon. We're part of a bigger company under Captain Jim Bridger. We're on our way now to meet up with him at Horse Creek—once we regroup with the rest of our company."

"Jim Bridger?"

"Know him?"

Petey Pauly was silent a moment. "Heard of him. Say, ye got a name, hoss?"

"It's Carson. Christopher Carson, but folks just generally call me Kit."

Another long silent spell passed. Kit tried to catch a glimpse of Meek and Gray Feather. He did not see them, but he had not really expected to. Experienced mountaineers both, they'd not give away their position when stalking quarry.

Pauly spoke from a new place among the rocks. "Don't reckon I ever heard your name spoke."

"Whal, come on down out of those rocks and we'll talk a spell." Kit started slowly out of his saddle.

"Betsy here ain't ready to palaver, stranger," Pauly shot back. "Moccasins touch ground and you'll go under, that's what she tells me."

Kit settled back into his saddle, impatience edging his voice now. "You won't let us ride away and you aren't gonna let us light. Make up your mind what you want, Pauly. Me and the boys need to find a place to spread our bedrolls soon."

"Tell me of the Blackfeet. Where did ye see them red devils?"

"Northwest of here. Near the Gallatin."

"Were they hauling plews?"

"Can't say. Never got a close enough look."

All at once Petey's rifle boomed. Kit flinched as a puff of gray smoke billowed above one of the distant rocks. The sounds of a struggle reached Kit's ears as he leaped to the ground. The next instant Meek and Gray Feather appeared, holding a wiry fellow at rifle point. They marched him down the rock slope into his camp.

The trappers all dismounted and gathered around Petey Pauly. The man seemed to shrivel beneath their fierce stares.

"Ye got me cold, hoss. Reckon I'm gone beaver," Pauly lamented.

"No one's gonna hurt you." Kit nodded at Gray Feather, and the Ute thrust Petey's empty rifle into the scrawny trapper's hands.

"You alone up here?" Kit asked.

Petey gently stroked the rifle as if it were a living thing with feelings and somehow he was trying to console it. "It's all right, Betsy. I'll take care of ye."

Pauly was of an indeterminable age. He did not look to be old, yet his bulging eyes in their receded sockets seemed to reflect great age. His beard was long and unkempt, still dark but marked here and there by long, tangled strands of white. His cheeks were sunken and the veins in his neck stood out as if he had not had a substantial meal in months, yet there was strength in his hands where they wrapped solidly around the rifle—an early Hawken that still used a flintlock. This fellow had not been back to St. Louis in some time, Kit surmised. Most everyone who had had converted their rifles over to the new caplock system, which was immensely more reliable, especially in wet weather.

Kit told his men to make camp. He was going to spend the night here in spite of any complaints that Petey Pauly might make. When the trappers had drifted off, Petey relaxed a mite, but he was still wary. Kit repeated his question.

"No, I'm not alone. Thar's my horse over thar. Are ye blind?"

"Just you and the horse?"

He gave Kit a withering stare. "No sir, no siree. Ebenezer is off somewhere, but he'll be back directly." A curious smile briefly lifted the corners of Petey's mouth.

"Ebenezer is your partner?"

"He is." The smile widened. "And he'll be right displeased if ye hurt me."

"We ain't gonna hurt you." Kit inclined his head at the fire pit. "Is that coffee you got warming thar?"

"Coffee? Shucks no, Carson. I ain't had me a taste of coffee in . . . in a coon's age. I can't remember how long it's been since I run out. I've been roasting acorns and grinding them in my coffee grinder. Say, ye wouldn't have any coffee with ye?"

"We have coffee," Kit said.

Pete grinned happily. "Maybe ye boys showin' up weren't such a bad thing after all. Leastwise, ye ain't gonna be able to steal my plews."

That was the second time he'd mentioned them making off with his winter's take. "What makes you say that?"

Petey frowned, then gave out with that cackling laugh again. " 'Cause the Blackfeet already been through here and done stole 'em! Took my extra horses, too. Lucky for me I was off tending my traps or they'd have lifted this child's scalp sure 'nough. Why, if Ebenezer had been around camp, them Injuns would be singing a different tune. Ebenezer hates Injuns, ye see." He slanted an eye in Gray Feather's direction. "Blackfeet put an arrow in his hide once, ye see. He don't like no Injun."

"How long ago were they through here?" The small stirrings of worry began to shoulder its way into Kit's brain. He thought of Huntington and his men, and of the Blackfeet who had mysteriously disappeared the day the two companies had split.

"Oh, four or six days ago," Petey answered. "Fact, when I heard your horses coming down the trail I suspicioned it might be them Injuns returning. That's why I skedaddle into them rocks. Of course, when I seen it was white men . . . mostly," he added, glancing again at Gray Feather, "I figured ye might be out to steal what the Injuns had left behind, which wasn't much." He wagged his bony head. "Where is Ebenezer when I need him?" Petey lamented.

Kit said, "You don't have to worry about us taking your belongings, Petey. We're on our way to the rend'vous, just as soon as we join up with the rest of our company."

"Rendezvous?" Petey chewed his cheek as if struggling to grab hold of a thought. "Say, whar might that be this year?"

"Horse Creek."

"I thought it was on the Skiskeedee?"

"That was the '34 meeting," Kit told him.

" 'Thirty-four?" Petey narrowed his left eye and stared at Kit. "What year is this?"

Gray Feather said, "It's 1836."

" 'Thirty-six!" Petey's mouth dropped a notch. "Ye mean to tell me I've been out here three winters already?"

"I don't know. You tell me how long you've been up here."

"I come out . . . I come out . . . ?" He had trouble recalling. "It was '33 I think or was it '32?"

"That would make it three or four years," Gray Feather allowed.

"Saints Almighty! Three years of working all by my lonesome in this land, and them Injuns got away with all of it!"

"Alone? What about Ebenezer?" Kit asked.

"Oh, yeah, Ebenezer. I forgot about him."

"By the way, you never did say where your partner was."

"I don't know where he is, Carson." Petey waved a bony hand toward the forest surrounding them. "He's around somewhere. He'll be back here in his own good time. That's just the way Ebenezer is." The loner fell into a deep funk and skulked to his lean-to, dragging Betsy behind him. He sat upon the crumpled blankets, cradled the rifle on his lap, and stared at the circle of blackened rocks where the camp-keeper, Franklin, was remaking the fire and putting on a pot of coffee.

Petey didn't blink an eyelash until dusk began to darken the land. Then, suddenly coming out of his trance, he stood and bent over the fire, drawing the odor of boiling coffee deep into his lungs. With each long inhalation, his spirits seemed to lift a little bit more until finally the codger was standing tall and grinning.

The camp-keeper dished up supper, and while the trappers sat around eating, Petey wandered off to the rocks where he had hidden earlier and sat alone in the growing gloom, eating and sipping his coffee with obvious delight.

Meek nodded toward Petey and said, "Looks like somebody done stole that child's rudder."

Menard, one of the trappers, chuckled and added, "His memory is dim as an old buffler trail."

The trappers had themselves a laugh.

Gray Feather said, "He's been alone for three or four years. A man who hasn't spoken with anyone for that long is bound to act queer."

"What about this partner of his, Ebenezer?"

Kit said, "If you ask me, I'd say Ebenezer is just someone he made up in his head."

Gray Feather told them of similar accounts he had read of people left alone for long periods of time developing imaginary friends.

"Reckon that him being alone all those years would addle his think box?" Franklin asked.

"These mountains can do it to a man," Kit answered.

"Whal, they sure seemed to have done it to that coon," Meek decided.

Petey came from the shadows and refilled his coffee cup from the pot on the fire. "This is the finest coffee I ever drunk!" he declared. "Roasted acorns don't shine a'all compared to the real stuff. And juniper tea is a poor substitute for even the worst-tastin' coffee. I can't remember how long it's been since I reached the bottom of my bean bag. And I ain't had a sip of whiskey since Ebenezer went an' drunk it all up on me. Say, ye boys wouldn't happen to have a sip of John Barleycorn with ye?"

"A jug of whiskey wouldn't last long in this company," Kit assured Petey. "We're dry as a bone whistle. But come rend'vous time there'll be enough ale and whiskey on hand to keep a monastery grinning."

"Hmm. Whar did ye say this year's gathering was gonna be?"

"The mouth of Horse Creek," Menard said. "Same place as last year."

"Reckon I must have missed last year's gathering."

There was no "reckoning" about it. Kit would have remembered Petey if he'd been at any of the rendezvous where he had set up his tent. "Where was your last meeting, Petey?"

Petey thought a moment, then said, "Don't reckon I ever been, Carson. I heard tell of it, though, from a couple of trappers who come through here a few years back."

Kit said, "How have you managed to keep your scalp, out here all alone?"

"I ain't alone," Petey replied. "Ebenezer is about somewhere. He'll be back directly. As far as this child's scalp is concerned, the Crows leave me alone. They call me Bear Man and ride wide of my camp. And up till a few days ago, I've managed to stand clear of the Blackfeet. But now that they've found me out, reckon I'm gonna have to up and move camp." He shook his head dourly. "Had me a passel of plews before they come through. I'd 've had me a pocketful of sovereigns if I could a taken them beaver to market. Looks like I'm gonna have to start all over again." He thought silently for a while, then drew in a long breath, heaving his bony shoulders. "Whal, looks like it'll be another five or six years before I get back to my Bernice, but she'll be so proud of her Petey when I do . . . that is, if she ain't already gone and got herself married again. I'll have coins in my pockets! Maybe I'll buy me a farm somewhar."

"I hear Oregon shines," Meek told him. "Someday I intend to mosey on over these mountains and settle thar. Maybe on the Columbia."

"Oreegon, ye say?"

Kit said, "Oregon needs Americans to move in, lots of 'em before it's lost to the British, who have thar own eyes on the place."

"Hmm. Whal, I just might give it a thought."

A rustling of pine needles out in the darkening forest brought Kit suddenly alert. Gray Feather and Meek had heard it too.

Kit reached for his rifle. All around him the trappers' talk went silent as each man's attention was suddenly focused on the sound of movement emerging from the deepening shadows. Only Petey seemed unconcerned.

"Bug's Boys?" Menard whispered.

"They could have come back," Franklin said.

Kit glanced at the lock of his rifle, checking that the cap was in place. He hooked a thumb over the hammer spur and stood, stepping out of the firelight. "It doesn't sound right, boys," he whispered. "Injuns wouldn't make that much noise."

"Kit's right," Gray Feather said. "If it was Blackfeet, we wouldn't hear them until they attacked."

"That's probably just Ebenezer coming back. He's a little shy around strangers."

"Ebenezer sure isn't light on his feet," Kit noted warily.

Petey cackled as if Kit had just told the most hilarious joke that he had heard in a long time—and perhaps he had.

The trappers weren't buying Petey's explanation so easily. They had taken up rifles and had put their backs together into a defensive circle, like Kit had seen mountain men do a time or two at a Taos fandango when the local boys got in a stew over the attention the trappers had been giving the pretty senoritas.

Heavy footsteps crashed to Kit's left. He swung his rifle, a spider crawling up his spine. If it was Ebenezer, the fellow must have weighed six hundred pounds or more!

Suddenly the evening stillness was shattered by a rumbling roar. It was a bear, Kit realized all at once. A grizzly, by the sound of it. The men swung their rifles toward the sound. A branch snapped underfoot. The bear was coming into camp.

In a shambling gait the bear lumbered into view. As Kit had feared, it was a huge, silver-tipped white bear. It gave forth a warning roar and instantly rose on his hind legs, towering nine feet above them.

Kit threw his rifle to his shoulder, but before his finger even curled around the trigger, Petey had leaped to his feet, moving like a barefooted man on a bed of coals. The scrawny trapper cried "No!" and flung himself in front of the growling monster, flinging his arms wide like a mother shielding her children from a band of renegade Comanches!

"What's that crazy coot doing?" Meek cried, narrowing an eye along the barrel of his rifle.

Just then one of the grizzly's huge paws, its glistening claws gleaming in the failing light, swept down on Petey's shoulder.

Chapter Four

It happened so fast, the trappers could only watch. Kit thought it peculiar that Petey would be waving his arms and imploring the men not to shoot. At first the men held back, fearing a bullet fired now might strike the crazy coot, but after a moment it became clear that Petey was not being mauled. Indeed, it was just the opposite. Petey was desperately attempting to protect the growling monster. Kit had watched in horror as the huge claw had swept down, but instead of swiping Petey's head off his shoulder as he had fully expected it to do, the massive appendage merely settled gently on the man's shoulder.

None of it made sense to Kit. Any sane man would be turning tail and running away, or trying to fill the bear with hot lead. The scene was so absolutely startling and foreign to anything the mountain men had ever witnessed that luckily not one of them fired a shot. And that was partly because, Kit decided, Petey was crying frantically, "Don't shoot, don't shoot!"

When after a few moments, against all reasoning, it became apparent that Petey was in no immediate danger, the trappers slowly lowered their rifles.

Petey continued hopping around like a man with a bad case of the collywobbles and no place to squat.

"Dadburn you, hosses, put them pieces down," Petey ordered.

The rifles slowly found their way into the crook of the trapper's arms, but no man there was about to unburden themselves from their weapons or let their trigger fingers drift.

The bear dropped back down to all fours and stuck his huge muzzle under Petey's armpit. Its large brown eyes stared at the trappers with a look that fell somewhere between curiosity and warning. The grizzly gave forth another forest-shaking roar. Saliva dripped from its great snarling fangs. Kit had the distinct feeling that if Petey had not been between them and the bear, blood and fur would be flying right now.

Kit said, "Hold your fire, boys."

Petey patted the bear's broad head and cooed, "It's all right, Ebenezer. These hosses ain't gonna hurt ye. Ye just gave them a start, that's all. Ain't that right, Carson? Ye ain't gonna use them rifles, are ye?"

Kit wasn't sure yet. He remembered a time he had been run up a tree by a pair of grizzlies, and recalled a few other encounters so close as to practically give *him* the collywobbles just thinking about it.

"Whal, tell him ye ain't gonna shoot him," Petey

pressed. "Good grief, hoss, ye don't want to make Ebenezer nervous, do ye?"

"Me make *him* nervous?" Kit blurted, hardly believing what he had heard.

Ebenezer roared.

The mountain men scrambled back a few steps.

Joe Meek glanced nervously at Kit. "Either say it, Kit, or let me put a bullet in that b'ar."

Kit had seen Meek go up against Blackfeet, Arapahos, and even fierce Diggers with more aplomb than he was showing now.

"Say what?" Kit demanded.

"That ye are friendly critters. What else? Ebenezer don't know your intentions, and ye don't want him to start to thinkin' of ye as Injuns now."

Gray Feather gulped and cast a glance at Manhead. The Delaware's trigger finger was still folded through the guard of his rifle, and there was a no-nonsense look of determination in the Indian's eyes. "You better say something quick, Kit," he urged.

This was preposterous! Kit didn't talk to bears, especially those unpredictable silver-tipped cousins of the grizzly variety. Every instinct within him cried out that these were critters to avoid at all costs . . . and to be killed whenever that first option was not available! Not to appease into being friendly!

Petey was becoming more agitated. "Dadgum ye, hoss, Ebenezer don't know if he ought to let ye stay or drive ye off. Better say something friendly while ye still got a chance!"

"Whal . . . what the blazes am I suppose to tell him?" Kit stammered, feeling foolish yet knowing that every man there was teetering on a narrow rail, not knowing if they should shoot or jump.

"Tell him you aren't going to hurt him," Gray Feather suggested.

Kit stared at his partner. "You think that b'ar understands American?"

"No, but he understands the tone of your voice."

Kit could be just stubborn enough about this to get a lot of people hurt. He didn't want that. Pride stayed his tongue a moment longer. Meek urged him to say *something*.

"Whal, all right, I'll do it a try if you think it will help." He looked at the bear, and in spite the absurdity of it all, he said, "You keep back from my boys, Ebenezer, and we'll stay clear of you. Deal?"

Petey petted the broad head again and said, "Thar, ye heard it straight from Carson's own mouth. They're friends now. Don't go givin' these hosses any more fright."

As if he understood, the bear shook its head free of Petey's touch and lumbered across the codger's campsite. The trappers went straight as a ramrod as the grizzly came near and cautiously sniffed their moccasins. Petey cackled in delight when it came to Gray Feather's turn. The powerful grizzly stopped and snarled.

Petey barked a sharp reprimand.

Ebenezer seemed uncertain about this one. He sniffed Gray Feather's feet and legs one more time, as if recording his peculiar odor for future reference, and went on to Kit, Meek, Archuleta, and Menard.

"I thought you said he hated Indians?" Gray Feather breathed out in a long sigh of relief after the bear had passed him by.

"It must be your father's white blood," Kit replied.

"It ain't that. Ye've spent too much time with white men," Petey said. "Ye've started to smell like one. Ebenezer ain't sure about ye. Don't go and get too near to him without me being nearby."

As with Gray Feather, the bear gave Manhead a long, burning stare. Then he snarled and Kit heard the muffled rattle of rifles being taken up again. Petey barked out another sharp reprimand to the bear. Giving a shake of his massive head, Ebenezer reluctantly passed Manhead by and continued to examine Franklin. When he had finished he lumbered off into the forest. But the big grizzly came back shortly, sniffed around the perimeter of the campsite, then curled up against a tree trunk and went to sleep. It took the trappers a mite longer to adjust to the bear among them than it did for Ebenezer to accept and then ignore the trappers.

Later, while the men were seated around the fire, talking, smoking, reading, settling in for the night, Kit and Meek hashed over plans for the next few days until they met up with Huntington. Kit saw that Petey was listening intently to their talk and their reminiscing of past rendezvous. Petey was particularly enthralled with a story Meek told Carlos Archuleta about the summer before, when Kit had confronted a troublemaking Frenchman named Shunar. Kit had fought a duel with the giant of a man on horseback and had put a pistol ball through the big fellow's arm. It did not kill Shunar, but it did silence his bothersome mouth for the remainder of the gathering.

"They fought over a young Arapaho squaw, a pretty little gal named Waa-nibe. Ain't that right, Kit?" Meek said, giving the trapper a knowing wink.

Kit had all he could do to hold back a blush. It was true, Waa-nibe—or Singing Grass as her name meant in English—and Kit had been seeing each other, growing closer, but he did not care to have the details of his personal romances made known to everyone there.

"Shunar had a bothersome mouth and he hated all Americans," Kit replied flatly. "It just so happened I was the one who shut it." And that was all Kit intended to say about the matter.

"These Company people who come from back east, they bring lots of whiskey with them, don't they?" Petey asked when Meek's yarn had run its course.

"Whiskey? Why, I would say so. I'd reckon thar's more 'an a dozen hogshead of fine sipping whiskey from each company at least," Meek proclaimed. "And nary more than a pint or two of it ever makes the return trip to St. Louie!"

Petey licked his lips. His gaze grew suddenly distant; a yearning, hungry look softened his face.

Kit said, "You been a long season alone in these mountains, Petey."

"That's the straight of it, Carson."

"You ever consider coming down for a month or so? It's not but a few easy days' march to the south of here to the mouth of Horse Creek—why, a man could even make it in one hard push, if he wanted to."

Petey absently twisted a long hank of his beard around his finger as he stared into the dark forest as if seeing something out there. "I used to think about it some, hoss." He said it quietly, almost as if speaking to himself. "But after a while, I just sort of forgot about the other people—except for the Injuns, that is. Can't never forget them lest ye lose your scalp."

Gray Feather had moved his thick book of Shakespeare onto his lap, but didn't open it yet. Instead he said, "The Blackfeet took your horses and pelts, you're out of coffee, sugar, flour, and tobacco. Probably low on powder and lead as well. Why don't you come along with us? At the very least you'll want to resupply yourself before trying to make up for your losses."

"I don't have nothing to trade for supplies with. They took everything I worked for. All I got left is one horse, a few traps what still work, this old iron Dutch oven, and a coffeepot. And Betsy, of course," he added, glancing affectionately to the rifle leaning against a nearby tree.

Gray Feather's hand slipped momentarily to the heavy pouch that he wore at his side. His fingers folded around it, around the gold coins that he'd been saving.

"I could stake you."

Petey looked up at him. "Ye'd do that? Stake a white man?"

Kit said, "Or you could sign on with one of the companies. They'd give you equipment to get back on your feet."

"I'm a free trapper, Carson," Petey shot back, pride suddenly in his voice. "I don't work for no company. No sir, I work for myself and that's all." He paused, and scratched the chin hidden somewhere beneath the long beard. His view hitched back around toward Gray Feather. "I appreciate the offer, Injun, but I'm not one to take charity."

"It's not charity," Gray Feather told him. "It's a business deal."

"Business?"

"Certainly. I lend you enough money to get you back on your feet this year. Next year when you sell your skins, you pay me back with interest."

"Interest?" His eyes compressed suspiciously. "What's this 'interest' ye're talking about?"

"Well, let's say I give you enough money to outfit

yourself for one year. At the end of that year, you return the money that I lent to you, and give me a new rifle too. That rifle is the interest you've paid on the loan."

"Give ye a rifle? Then ye'd have two rifles. What do ye need two rifles for? One of 'em would just get in the way."

"I don't need two rifles. I'd sell one of them."

"Hmm." Petey pondered this a moment. "If ye did so, ye'd have more gold than ye started with."

"Precisely. And that is what makes this a business deal."

Petey's forehead wrinkled, his brain attempting to grasp the implication of what Gray Feather was trying to tell him. "That ain't nothing like charity," he finally decided.

"Not at all. It's how men conduct business."

"Hmm. I'm gonna have to think on this awhile."

"Certainly. Now, can I ask you a question?"

"Shoot, hoss."

"Why does Ebenezer hate Indians?"

"I already said why. One of them varmints went and put a arrow into his hide when he was but a cub. They done it after them red devils went and kilt his mama. I come along and nursed the tyke back to health. And lucky for me I did. Ol' Ebenezer thar has yanked my fat from out of the fire a time or two, he has. That's why the Crows leave me alone now. Why they call me Bear Man. I'm bad medicine to the Crow." He shook his head and gave a short laugh. "Too bad the Crows and Blackfeet are such enemies. Maybe if they was on more friendly terms, Bug's Boys would have heard of my fierce reputation and have left me alone."

Kit laughed.

Gray Feather grinned and said, "Well, you sleep on the offer, Petey," and opened the heavy tome upon his lap and tilted it slightly toward the firelight.

"Say, what's that ye're reading thar, hoss?"

Gray Feather glanced up. "*The Merchant of Venice.* It's one of the Shakespearean comedies, although many scholars consider it serious drama because the story is character driven rather than plot driven."

Petey scratched his head, his bulging eyes shining yellow in the dancing light of the fire. "Whar did a Injun ever learn to read that stuff?"

"Harvard College."

"Harvard College! Why, if ye ain't the oddest Injun I ever did meet."

Kit Carson roused the trappers early the next morning, but it wasn't early enough to beat Ebenezer out of bed. The grizzly had obviously awakened before them and had already left the campsite. And that was just fine with Kit. He bent over the place where the bear had slept, felt the warmth still in the matted pine needles. Petey's pet grizzly had only very recently gone off. As far as Kit was concerned, if the bear never came back he'd be happy. He glanced at Petey, who was hovering like a turkey vulture near the cook fire, anticipating the pot of coffee beginning to steam there.

Although Kit held no love for grizzly bears, he knew that Petey would miss Ebenezer when the day came for them to part company, and that day would surely come. The bear had been his only real companion for years. Petey probably owed his survival in this harsh wilderness to the fondness the bear showed him, and to the superstitions that had arisen among the Crow Indians about the strange relationship.

When it became apparent to Petey that the trappers were going to pull out, he grabbed Betsy by the barrel and strolled over to Kit, trailing the rifle behind him.

"Did ye mean what ye said yesterday, hoss?"

Kit was rolling his blankets into their oilcloth covering. He looked up from his task. "About you riding along with us to Horse Creek? I meant it."

Petey dragged the tip of his tongue across his cracked lips. Kit sensed that there were some real doubts worrying the man, not the least of them being whether or not he was ready to mingle with a great number of people again. Solitude, when endured long enough, can become a rather comfortable ball and chain.

Petey hesitated. "Whal, I've been giving it some thought, Carson." He let that statement hang there for a while.

"And?" Kit prompted, watching the indecision in Petey's bulging eyes.

"If ye give me time to collect in my traps and get my things together, I'll take up the offer."

Kit thought it over. He didn't expect Huntington and his men to be at the spouting fountains yet, and another few days of waiting here would be no worse nor no better than waiting there. "We've got some time to whittle on, Petey. I reckon another day or two won't matter now. Go on and do what you have to."

Petey grinned. "Ye are some, hoss. I'll get to my traps today, collect 'em up, and work what beaver there might be in them." Still grinning, Petey bobbed his head two or three times, then hotfooted it back to the cook fire to wait for the first cup of coffee from it.

"What was that all about?" Joe Meek asked, suddenly standing behind Kit. Meek had arrived with a soft-footed silence, a peculiar trait of the men who had survived wilderness living for very many years.

"Petey has decided to ride along with us to Horse Creek. I told him we would stay here another day or two while he brings in his traps."

Meek gave a laugh. "So that old fool is going to come out of these hills for a spell after all."

Kit looked around the camp and, not seeing the grizzly anywhere, said, "I just hope his *partner* doesn't decide to tag along too."

Meek's grin reversed itself. "If that b'ar shows up at rendezvous, he'll be stew meat and axle grease before the first week is over. Especially if Ebenezer really does have a taste for Injun blood. Rocky Mountain boys don't shine to the sort of nonsense we're putting up with here, Kit. I don't care how friendly the critter is."

Kit had to agree. He'd have to tell Petey to leave the bear behind. He was pretty certain Petey would understand. What worried him was how Ebenezer would take the news.

Chapter Five

The trappers took to lazing around Petey's campsite an extra day or two like bucks to a salt lick. Not a man among them lifted a voice to challenge Kit's decision. The weather was warm, the valley was protected, running water was nearby, and fresh game was plentiful.

For the winter-weary trappers it was a time to stitch up open seams, to make new moccasins, to draw the blade of a well-used butcher knife across a whetstone in a leisurely fashion. Some, like Franklin, wrote in their journals. Some clawed and shaped soft bar lead into swaged bullets. Some just lay back thinking about the pretty Indian girls who would populate the rendezvous in ample number just a few weeks from today. Others, like Kit, used the time to disassemble their rifle and carefully clean and oil each part of it. Gray Feather, as usual whenever he found a few minutes of respite from the demanding work of trapping, either scribbled notes in his leather-bound journal or opened a book and lost himself in reading.

Petey had gone off to collect his traps and any beaver they might have caught since the previous afternoon when he had last tended to them. Normally a trapper would have checked them that same night, but Petey had been distracted by the arrival of Kit and the other mountain men.

The morning passed quietly and congenially. Joe Meek, as ever, was spinning a yarn, this time a story about one night when he and a fellow named Reese were on night guard in Blackfoot country, very near to this place they were today. Meek and Reese had fallen asleep while on duty.

"Sublette come from his tent during the night and gave out a call to his guards. When he got no reply he strode toward the horse pens swearing and snortin', and lookin' for us. Sublette war powerful mad," Meek said. "He made enough noise to awaken Reese, who, immediately understanding the trouble he war in, whispered to Sublette, 'Down, Billy! Injuns!' Sublette dropped in his tracks and whispered, 'Whar is Meek?' 'Trying to shoot one of 'em,' Reese replied. Then Reese crawled off and woke me and told me the fix we war in. So I agreed to pretend along with Reese's story. In a little while I crawled back to where Reese and Sublette war. Sublette asked how many there war. I told him I didn't get a count. The next morning Sublette found an Injun moccasin print—I made certain he would. Whal, instead of being called down for our napping, we war called heroes and Sublette admired us both for our vigilance."

The trappers had themselves a chuckle over how Meek had fooled the big booshway—the company leader—and Kit said, "I'll remember that story the next time you do night guard for me."

"I was a green coon back then, Kit. This child don't sleep when on night guard no more."

No sooner had the low tittering died down than Franklin looked up from his writing and stared suddenly at the forest. "Oh, oh, trouble comes this way, boys."

They craned their heads around as Ebenezer plodded from the trees and strolled casually into camp.

"Where is that crazy coot when we need him?" Menard said, eyeing the grizzly warily.

Manhead reached for his rifle. "What worry you, white man? It is Delaware that bear hates."

Gray Feather, siting on the ground with his legs stretched out in front of him, had been reading aloud to three other trappers. He stopped and set the book down now. The bear sniffed at Petey's blankets, then turned back and recrossed the campsite, its weak eyes shifting back and forth as if searching for something—or someone. When it neared Gray Feather, the bear stopped suddenly and carefully sniffed at the sole of his moccasin. Gray Feather carefully drew his legs up beneath him.

"He taking a special interest in you," Archuleta said under his breath.

Gray Feather cast about for his rifle, which was leaning against a tree trunk beyond his reach. But already a half-dozen rifles had been taken up and the entire camp was poised to act quickly if it looked like the bear might attack.

Ebenezer growled.

Hammers clicked back to full cock.

Gray Feather said, "Shoo. Go away. Go bother Manhead!"

"Thank you, brother," Manhead said from across the way.

Gray Feather knew that to show fear was a sure way to embolden a grizzly. "What's with you, bear? Can't you understand English? I said be gone!"

Ebenezer cocked his head, his lips curling back, exposing great, curving fangs.

Kit slowly brought up his rifle and narrowed an eye along its long barrel.

"Just give the word, Kit," Meek said, snuggling his own rifle, which he affectionately called Sally, tight into his shoulder.

"Maybe he wants to hear the story too?" Archuleta suggested as he eased a pistol from his belt.

Gray Feather stared the bear in the eyes. "Is that what you want? You want to be read to? Well, you can't frighten me." In spite of his mounting trepidation, Gray Feather forced his eyes back to the book and began to read aloud. He struggled at first for a deep, confident voice, and after a minute the words began to flow again. Purposefully Gray Feather ignored the bear. He was determined not to allow fear to show through his bold and deceptive exterior.

Ebenezer stood there, small eyes peering hard at the Ute Indian. Gray Feather read on. The bear cocked his head to one side. Minutes passed. Except for Gray Feather's voice ringing out the words that William Shakespeare had penned centuries earlier, there was not another sound in the camp. With their rifles ready for instant action, the trappers waited to see what would happen next.

And what happened next was that Ebenezer suddenly sat down. The bear seemed enthralled. Kit was amazed. He had to conclude it was the rhythm of the words and the sound of the Indian's voice that had captivated Ebenezer's attention.

More minutes passed. The trappers slowly lowered their weapons as they watched the bear, planted solidly at Gray Feather's feet, listening to the words spilling forth.

"Now, there's a tale for you, Joe," Menard said to Meek.

The seasoned mountain man only shook his head. "No, Antoine, no one would ever believe it."

Gray Feather read and read until he was hoarse and his throat began to tighten up on him, yet he kept at it, fearing what Ebenezer would do if he stopped. But there came a point when he could go no further. He arrived at the end of Act II and closed the book. "That's it. That's all I can do," he told the bear. Now shoo!"

Obediently, the bear stood and lumbered off.

Not a man there spoke. Archuleta could only shake his head. Meek, for the first time that Kit could remember, was speechless. Kit found his voice finally and said, "Maybe we ought to start calling Gray Feather 'Bear Man'."

"Thanks, but no thanks. That dubious honor can remain with Petey. The sooner we're away from that monster, the better I'll like it." Gray Feather watched Ebenezer stroll casually off into the forest. When the bear had gone, the Ute shuddered as if a cold wind had suddenly blown past. He set the book aside and went down to the stream for a long cool drink to soothe his weary vocal cords.

The next day the men were back on the trail.

Petey had collected his gear and Kit had lent him a spare horse to pack it out on. Kit led the party west, watching for the landmarks that would steer him straight toward the spouting fountain. The spouting fountain was a spectacular geyser that discharged a spout of hot water at such regular intervals that a man might regulate his chronometer to it—if any man there owned a chronometer. Such fragile devices were wholly impractical and quite useless for mountain living.

They traveled past steaming cracks and boiling mud. Meek was on the lookout for his foe with the tail and pitchfork. Vast herds of buffalo wandered through the area. Kit read the tracks of bear and mountain lion, deer, elk, and wolf. This steaming land teemed with life. It was a favorite home to an army of wild creatures during the long, frigid winters because water never froze in the hot, deep pools.

Thinking about that, Kit peered across the long valley they were crossing, which was greening up after the long winter. Ebenezer was there, maybe a quarter of a mile away, keeping pace with the party. Without wanting to, Kit frowned. He had told Petey before leaving camp that the bear would have to stay, but the codger had replied that Ebenezer goes generally where Ebenezer wishes to go, and generally where he wishes to go is where Petey goes.

There was no way any of the men knew of to make the bear stay behind . . . even if he had wanted to, which Petey had made quite clear that he did not. But he assured Kit that Ebenezer would behave himself at the rendezvous. Perhaps that was so. Kit, however, could not offer Petey the same assurance where the hundreds of gathering trappers and Indians were concerned.

"What's got you worried, Kit?" Gray Feather asked, riding up alongside his friend.

Kit looked over and erased the frown from his face. "Is it that plain?"

"Judging by those furrows cutting into your forehead a moment ago, I'd say something is weighing heavy on your brain." Gray Feather checked the direction Kit had been looking and briefly watched the bear at the far edge of the valley. "And if I don't miss my guess, I'd say that something has to do with about nine hundred pounds of muscle and fur."

"I ain't got any love for grizzlies, Gray Feather. But Ebenezer is a critter cut from a different bolt than the rest. Him and Petey take care of each other. I'd not like to see the b'ar go under, but I fear that's just what will happen if he shows up at rend'vous."

"That bear showing up or not showing up is out of your hands. There isn't anything you can do to change what will happen, Kit. Besides," Gray Feather offered reasonably, "maybe nothing will happen at all."

Gray Feather was only trying to help, but his words did not make Kit feel any easier about the impending demise of the friendly bear. "I know what you're trying to say, but you know as well as me that thar will be a passel of Injuns at Horse Creek, and a couple hunder' Rocky Mountain boys. How long do you figure it'll be before that b'ar decides to have himself a taste of Injun blood? And even if he does manage to behave himself, how long before someone takes a pint too much whiskey and gets to eyeing up a new b'arskin robe for his sweetheart?"

The day lengthened as the trappers drew closer to the spouting fountain where they were to meet Huntington and the rest of the company. Kit had tarried long enough to give Jim Huntington enough time to make the journey from the Jefferson River, where the last cache of furs had been hidden, to this meeting place.

As he rode, Kit tried not to think about Petey or the bear, and instead he turned his musings to the reunion with Huntington, the rejoining of their forces, and the short ride afterward to this year's rendezvous. It was an easy two- or three-day journey to the mouth of Horse Creek and festive get-together of mountain men from all over the territory; from as far away as the British colonies up north, to the Mexican lands down south . . . even some all the way from Spanish California. It was an annual event few men ever missed on purpose. Those who did were immediately suspected of having met unfortunate circumstances and an early demise.

Spring was in its full glory in this land of weird contrasts, of steaming vents and boiling mud, and of peaceful deep blue lakes, roving buffalo, and shy deer. The grassy hillsides were freshening with new green, while streams pushed at their banks with the icy melt of vast snow sheets that still clung tight to the shady side of a valley or mountain peak.

Kit knew he was close to the spouting fountain when the forest began to thin up ahead. He was on the lookout for Huntington and his party. Huntington would more than likely choose to make his camp in the protection of the trees rather than out on the wide meadow. It was upon this meadow that the spouting fountain burst forth in a regular manner, as if far down below the surface of the earth a mighty pump was beating like a heart. Through the trees Kit had a glimpse of green. He cautiously approached the edge of the forest and brought the trappers to a halt.

Before them lay a pretty meadow of maybe a hundred acres where last year's dead grass was rapidly being replaced with fresh green shoots beneath a cloak of white and pink flowers. At its far end the land rose into several whitish knolls that contrasted starkly with the verdant swale that surrounded them. The forest resumed its march a few hundred feet beyond.

"Thar it is," Kit announced, pointing.

Archuleta peered ahead, skepticism plain upon his face. "All right, so why is it called the 'spouting fountain'? I do not see any water."

"You just wait," Meek told him. "Any minute now you'll see why it's called that. You best not be near that thing when it blows."

"Why's that?"

"Why? Whal, it'll boil you like a crawfish, that's why."

Archuleta still looked skeptical, as if he might be judging this to be just another of Meek's yarns.

Gray Feather said, "Let's move in closer, Kit."

But Kit held the party at the forest's edge a while longer as he scanned the line of trees that ringed this meadow. "I expect Huntington's arrived already. Wonder where him and the others have made camp." Although there had been no indication that anything had gone wrong, a note of concern was in his voice.

Meek said, "Maybe they're camped the other side of this here clearing, Kit. Beyond the fountain."

"Maybe," Kit allowed.

Petey said, "That's what I would do, not wanting to attract no Crows or Blackfeet visitors." He stood in his saddle and looked around the small party. "Wonder whar Ebenezer got off too."

High, thin clouds had drifted across the sky, muting the sun's sharp afternoon light. Now, as the men sat their horses out of sight of anyone who might be watching from the cover of the forest, the clouds drifted past and the greens and pinks and whites took on a sudden brilliance. The knolls at the far end gleamed as if wet, and now Kit saw that they were strangely mottled here and there with dark brown spots. He did not recall seeing those splotches the last time he had been through here. From this distance they reminded him of age spots on an old man's bald head.

Kit leaned forward, studying them. For some unknown reason a shiver stroked his spine. "Meek, what do you make of that?"

Joe shaded his eyes and squinted against the glare. He did not speak at once, and when he did there was a sudden wariness in his voice. "I don't like the looks of this, Kit."

Menard and Franklin brought their horses forward a few paces. "What is it? What do you see, Kit?" Menard asked. Kit pointed at the odd mottling, which was too far off to be seen clearly with the unaided eye.

Gray Feather fished around inside his saddlebag a moment and came up with his tattered leather-covered journal in which he recorded notes and snippets of his journeys. He had often proclaimed that someday he intended to write a history of these events. Gray Feather rolled a piece of paper between his palms, forming a long, thin tube. He put one end of it to his right eye, shutting the left.

"Kit, you better have a look at this." The sudden urgency in the Ute's voice was the confirmation Kit was hoping he would not hear.

The paper spyglass sharpened details by eliminating distractions, and cut out everything but the chalky formations in the distance. In spite of the distance, the objects came into sharp focus. A hollowness deepened within Kit's belly and his jaw took a firm set, his lips thinning to a bitter, hard slash across his face. "It's Huntington and his men."

Kit handed the paper tube to Meek. The mountain man squinted through it. "My Gawd," he croaked, passing it to Menard, who swallowed hard after taking a long look and handing the tube to Archuleta.

The makeshift spyglass made the rounds until everyone had had a look.

Kit checked the pistols in his belt and hitched his buffalo rifle under his arm. "Keep a sharp eye out, boys," he said, starting around the edge of the meadow but keeping within the cover of the trees. No one spoke. Some eyes were turned toward the clearing, others toward the deep forest. Every ear was alert for the slightest sound that would warn of an impending Indian attack.

As they drew nearer to the mounds, it became clear that their pasty color was due to a lack of vegetation and to whitish chemical deposits of some kind. The trappers had seen many deep-earth vents like these during the few days they had been in this strange, steaming land. Kit brought the party to a halt at a place where the forest nudged into the meadow close to the blanched mounds. Petey's unblinking eyes bulged at the bloody scene before them. Silence hung in the air like an omen of even worse things to come.

With faces cast into grim masks of fear and revulsion, the trappers left the cover of the trees and rode across the new grass to the mounds. Kit's stomach knotted at the sight before him. When he came to the first body, still several dozen feet from the spouting fountain, Kit reined to a halt and swung out of his saddle. He turned the man over. It was a fellow named Warren Canfield. Kit had to force himself to look at the corpse. Canfield had been sliced open from belly to brisket and his intestines spilled out upon the ground. They had taken his hair, and his skull bone looked oddly white in the late light. His genitals had been savagely hacked away.

Kit looked away, lifting his eyes to the mounds ahead where more bodies lay in the impossible but undeniable sprawl of death. Kit came upon four other men whom he knew; a fifth was beyond recognition. Upon the slick-rock slope of the mound he found more bodies. The arrows and the mutilations told the story. Even the horses had been shot. Presumably the trappers had tried to flee. A line of bodies led back toward the trees to the north. The attack had come from that direction. The trappers must have been taken by surprise. They had fled south, into the meadows, making a final stand here, on the slopes of the spouting fountain. Their clothing was soaked with water and blood had streamed down the sides of the mounds, staining the pale stone with red streaks.

Manhead discovered the body of Owl Man upon one of the mounds and fell to his knees at his cousin's side, gently placing a hand on the cold body. The Delaware said nothing, made no outward sign of emotion, but Kit noted the slight quiver in the Indian's stiffly held spine. It was not Manhead's way to outwardly display his feelings.

From the center of one of the largest mounds rose a steady cloud of steam. From its far side Meek's voice reached Kit. "I found Huntington," he said soberly.

Kit started across to him. Just then the ground beneath his feet started to tremble and a sound arising from deep within the earth began to rumble toward the surface.

"Take cover, men!" Kit shouted. "It's about to blow!" Kit dashed off the side of the mound, his long strides carrying him far into the grass a dozen yards off before turning back. When he did, Kit was stunned to discover that Archuleta was still standing near the vent, staring down into it, either in fascination or riveted there by fear.

"Carlos! Get clear of that thing!" Kit yelled, but the Mexican seemed not to hear.

Dropping his rifle and powder horn, Kit made a dash for the man.

Chapter Six

Kit raced up the side of the mound, hearing the deep rumbling beneath him growing louder, feeling the earth begin to shake. Any second now, he knew . . .

He snagged Archuleta by the arm.

"What?" Carlos said, startled. He looked vaguely confused, as if he had been lost in a thought.

"We got to get away from here now!"

The Mexican seemed to have been in a trance, stunned by the sight of the bodies, by the rumbling that now vibrated up through the soles of their moccasins. But when he saw the urgency in Kit's eyes, reality smacked him between the eyes. He spun about on his heels even as the rumbling beneath their feet rose to a crescendo and a fountain of steaming water shot from the crack at the center of the largest mound.

Both men ran for the grassy meadow beyond the

sloping white stone. Kit felt the heat upon his back as the scalding water spurted two hundred feet into the air. Some of it stung his neck and hands, and soaked into his buckskin shirt. But the two men cleared the fountain's reach by the time the bulk of the shooting water had fallen back to the ground.

Archuleta had awakened fully from his stupor by the time they reached safety. "That was a close one," he said.

"What war you thinking, Carlos?" Meek shouted above the roar of spouting water. "I warned you."

Archuleta managed a feeble grin. "I think maybe I was waiting to see if that fellow with the tail and pitchfork was a-coming."

"You might have seen him for a fact if Kit hadn't yanked you outta thar," Meek retorted.

The men backed farther from the fountain, watching its waters gush skyward. The spectacle of vaporous jets of steaming water shooting hundreds of feet into the air mingled with the roaring of steam and the trembling of the ground beneath them. The hot water rained down upon the bodies lying there. Rivulets of water tinted red brought fresh color to the dark streaks. The eruption lasted for four or five minutes, then slowly diminished until it finally disappeared, leaving the pale rock steaming from its heat.

"How often does it do that?" Archuleta asked when the display had ceased. There was a quiet awe in his voice that bordered on reverence.

"I don't know exactly," Kit said. "About once every hour, I'd guess."

"At least that often," Gray Feather affirmed.

"Often enough that when the ground begins to tremble and that crack takes to spittin', that's warning enough that you best hightail it to a safe distance."

The trappers took advantage of the interval between eruptions to remove the bodies from the mounds and take them back into the forest. They found Huntington's campsite and discovered that at least some of the horses had not been killed. The Blackfeet had stolen the horses carrying the packs of beaver pelts. Kit knew that had been the Indians' intention all along. It was why they had been followed, and why the Blackfeet had waited until the company had split and the numbers reduced. If Kit had taken the packhorses with him, it would have been he and his men who were murdered instead of Huntington and the trappers who had gone with him.

When all the bodies had been found and brought into the cover of the trees, there remained but one task left to do. "We best dig a grave for them," Kit said. His sober tone was reflected in the faces of the trappers standing there. Even the usually jovial Joe Meek was frowning darkly.

Meek, Archuleta, and Menard began digging a hole large enough to take all the bodies.

"Those red bastards did it for the plews," Franklin said. "What are we going to do about it, Kit?"

Kit saw that Franklin's question was weighing heavy on each man's mind. Kit noted that one of the men was missing. "Where's Gray Feather?"

Petey pointed off toward the east. "Me and Betsy seen him go off thataway," he said.

Manhead said, "You want I go look for him?"

Just then Gray Feather appeared through the trees. A man was hobbling at his side, using the Ute for support. Menard and Meek rushed to lend a hand with the wounded man.

Maximilian Overmier's face was pale from loss

of blood. A Blackfoot arrow protruded from his left leg; another had buried itself in his left side. Both wounds had stopped bleeding.

"It vas a horrible ting," Overmier said through gritted teeth after taking a long drink of water.

"How did it happen, Max?"

"They come of a sudden, Kit. Ve had no idea they vere even following us."

"When?"

Overmier took another drink. Pushing the tin cup away, he said, "It vas morning . . . this morning. Ve had just come avake and vere making a break fast."

"How many?"

Overmier shook his head. "Don't know. Many. Maybe thirty, maybe forty . . . maybe more. Huntington and the others, they make stand, but the savages drive him back. One, he come after me. I split his noggin with a rifle ball. Then two more come. Hit me once here. Again here. I crawl off and hide. Two or three come looking. Don't find. They go back and fight the others. I pass out. Ven I come to again it all over and I hurt too bad to move. Luck with me Gray Feather see my tracks, no?" He grinned at the Ute.

"You were lucky, I reckon." Kit frowned at the arrows driven deep into the German's flesh.

"Were them Blackfeet hauling plews with 'em?"

Overmier's blue eyes shifted, focusing on Petey. "Who are you?"

"Someone we picked up along the way," Kit told him. "He just lost his catch to a band of Blackfeet. Might be the same bunch who hit you."

Overmier shook his head. "Don't know about no plews. But I reckon they took all that ve vas carrying. More than a thousand pound's vorth, no?"

Kit nodded. "Least that much."

Overmier grimaced. "Damn them savages to hell! Kit, I could take another drink."

Kit brought the cup to Overmier's mouth. "You just relax now best you can, Max. I'll sharpen a knife and see about cutting those arrows out of your hide."

"They might be poisoned, Kit," Manhead said quietly when Kit left the wounded man.

"Maybe they are and maybe not. We won't know for a day or two. In the meanwhile, they still have to come out."

"What are we gonna do now, Kit? Seems to me we got to make a decision here," Joe Meek said later, after the bodies had been buried and the surgery on Overmier finished. The wounded man lay asleep beneath a buffalo robe.

Kit drew thoughtfully at the stem of his clay pipe and blew out a cloud of smoke. It swirled in the chill air before the firelight and dissipated against the dark forest beyond. Kit had a problem. A problem that he'd been pondering for most of fifteen minutes now. Meek's question merely put words to it.

"Whal," he began slowly, still groping for an answer. "The way I see it, we have three choices."

A long silence stretched out. Meek held his tongue and waited for Kit to put his thoughts into words. The tobacco in the bowl of Kit's pipe flared, casting a red light upon the mountain man's face.

"I've got a real powerful notion to go after those Injuns and punish them for what they done today."

"Every child here would stand behind you if you did, Kit. These were our friends."

"I know that, Joe."

"If you let Injuns go unpunished you're just encouraging them to do it again."

"I know that too."

"Then what's stopping us?"

"You mean what other than the fact that we'd be outnumbered six to one?"

Meek grimaced in the firelight. "Bug's Boys took Huntington by surprise. It's the only reason they got away with it. If we turn the tables on them, we can bloody their nose some."

Kit managed a fleeting grin. "We could at that." He'd take great satisfaction in bloodying the Blackfeet's noses after what they had done here today. "But that brings up the second dilemma."

"What might that be?"

Kit glanced up as Gray Feather joined them. The half-breed did not speak, but hunkered down, listening to their talk. Kit looked back at Joe Meek. "We're carrying three hundred pounds of beaver. That's a pitiful part of what we took in all winter, but still it figures out to something around twelve hundred dollars at rend'vous prices. I've got an obligation to the men, and to Bridger, to see that those plews get safely down to Horse Creek. If we light out after Blackfeet now, we risk losing them too."

"So our second choice is letting the savages go unpunished and taking what we can save of this disaster and hightailing it outta here."

"We've got Overmier to consider too. He can't join in a fight, and we can't leave him alone. Someone would have to stay with him. See that he gets down to the meeting. I hear that Doc Whitman is coming through again this year. He done a fine job of cutting that arrowhead out of Bridger's back last rend'vous. He could help Overmier now."

Meek had to admit that Kit had a point. "All right. I can see whar that's true. We need to think of Overmier, and we need to protect the plews we still have."

Each man pondered his own thoughts while out in the meadow the spouting fountain erupted again, filling the night with its roar as steaming hot water shot up into the night sky.

Meek said, "You said thar war three choices, as far as you could see. What's the third?"

Kit lowered his pipe and looked first at Gray Feather, then at Meek. "The third is this. You, Archuleta, Franklin and Petey take the plews and Overmier out of here. The rend'vous is south of here. By their signs, Bug's Boys went off to the north. You won't have any trouble with Injuns if you keep your wits about you. In two or three days you'll be safe at Horse Creek."

Joe Meek was frowning. Kit could see he wasn't favorably impressed with the idea. "And what will you, Gray Feather, Menard, and Manhead be doing while I'm running away to safety?"

"Yes, what about us, Kit?" Gray Feather asked.

"We'll be trailing those coons, Gray Feather. We'll find where thar camp is and take back those eight thousand dollars' worth of plews they took from us."

"No." Meek's eyes were intense. "I want a piece of them savages too." The sudden ardor in Meek's voice drew the attention of the men in camp and they came over to learn the cause of the outburst.

Kit spread out his plan before them. Franklin and Petey announced that they intended to go along with Kit too. Kit had the beginning of an insurrection here, so strongly did the men wish to punish the Blackfeet for their treachery. He had to extinguish it quickly.

Petey said, "I take orders from no man, Carson. I've a stake in this too, ye might remember. Them red critters took my horses and plews . . . took 'em first, they did, before they done the same to your boys here. I'll go with ye, and ye'll have to tie me to a tree to stop me if ye say no." His fist tightened around the rifle. "And Betsy here is of the same mind."

"I think we're all of that mind, Kit," Franklin added.

"But we can't all go," Kit pointed out. "Overmier needs care, and the few pelts we have left need to be protected. No matter how we cut the pie, boys, some of us will have to stay behind and some of us will go. The smart thing is for them who stay to take the plews and Overmier to safety."

"*Some of us* have never been accused of being awful smart, Kit," Meek said.

The men mumbled among themselves, but each knew that Kit was right. They could not all go after the Indians. At least one man would have to stay behind with Overmier. And if one man stayed, then he would need a partner, for a single healthy man with a wounded man was a sure ticket to a scalping party in this country, and they all knew it.

"Then I say we draw lots," Menard said.

"You leave me outta it." Petey scowled at Kit. "You coons can settle it among yourselves whatever way ye see fit. As for me, I'm going after them savages, and thar ain't a man here who can stop me."

"No drawing lots," Kit said, asserting his role as booshway of this small group. "I say who comes and I say who goes back. Any man here wants to go against that, stand forward now and make your case." His eyes hardened and turned on each of the trappers, locking on them a moment until they were compelled to look away.

Petey said, "Ye might be booshway to these men, hoss, but ye hold no rein over me."

"You're right, Petey, I don't. And if you want to come along I won't stop you. But bear in mind that if you do, you take orders from me. And if that's not to your liking, I *will* tie you to a tree before we pull up stakes."

Petey snorted his displeasure at the arrangement, but he agreed to it just the same. "Ye just be careful ye don't lead us into no ambush, hoss." He slung Betsy into the crook of his arm and sulked away.

"Friendly old coot, isn't he?" Archuleta observed.

Kit understood the loner's problem. After years living alone, Petey wasn't used to taking orders from any man, and it was hard for him to start doing so now. "He just needs to rub shoulders with his kind more often. Living a hermit's life out here all these years has soured him some."

"Soured him some?" Meek gave a short laugh. "He's a pickle, that one." The trapper's brief smile wilted and he narrowed a stern eye at Kit. "So, who goes and who stays?"

Meek was Kit's age, and the two of them had come to the mountains about the same time. Both men were qualified to lead this small company of trappers, but it was because of Kit's level head that Bridger had put *him* in charge of these men when they had split up after coming out of winter quarters. In the broad scheme of things, Bridger was the booshway and Kit was what was known as the little booshway. But since Bridger was presumably already at the Horse Creek rendezvous awaiting their return, Kit was in full charge here. And Meek was testing the waters to see just how much in charge Kit really was.

"Already told how it was going to be, Joe," Kit replied evenly, his eyes unflinching.

Meek's face hardened. But before he could protest further, Kit went on. "You and me, we've been in these mountains a long time, Joe. Seen us a lot of trouble, traded lead for arrows with most every hostile tribe out here." Kit inclined his head toward Archuleta and Franklin. "We have some men with us who are new to the mountain, who don't know the way of the Injuns like you and me know 'em. It would be downright reckless of me to give greenhorns the job of getting those pelts and Overmier safely out of here. You, on the other hand, got more mountain savvy than any ten men I know of. With you leading 'em I wouldn't have to worry about what's happening down the trail, Joe. I could think about getting our pelts back, and keeping our scalps in place. I need you with them more than I need you with me."

Meek scowled, but his fire cooled some. "If you aren't the grandest silver-tongued liar I ever did hear, Kit. Are all Missourians sech liars?"

Kit smiled. "And you're a Virginia gentleman in spite of all your bluster."

"All right. We'll do it your way. I'll see that Overmier and the plews get down to Horse Creek safe and sound." Meek's voice turned stern. "But as soon as I get thar I'm rounding me up half a hunder' Rocky Mountain boys and coming back a-looking for you."

Kit nodded. "You do that. About a half a hundred will be just about right, I reckon."

Meek grinned. "Don't punish them savages all by yourself, Kit. I want a piece of them in a real bad way."

"I'll leave a few for you to handle, Meek."

Meek nodded and snorted. "Just see to it that you do. Don't want you having all the fun."

The erupting geyser out in the meadow had fallen silent again, and suddenly a snap of a twig from deep in the forest riveted their attention. Their talking ceased, and quietly the trappers reached for their weapons, putting distance between each other just in case . . .

But it was only Ebenezer finally coming in to visit. The bear had followed the company at a distance all that day, and for a while at least, Kit had not thought about the grizzly. Finding Huntington's party and burying them in a single grave had pushed the minor annoyance of a friendly grizzly bear to the back of his brain.

Still wary of the docile monster, the trappers relaxed at his appearance, but they kept their rifles within quick reach. Kit was relieved that it was only the bear and not the Blackfeet coming to call again. Not that he had expected the Indians to return tonight. Just the same, Kit set up a rotation of guards for the night.

But with Ebenezer lingering nearby, Kit felt strangely at ease this night. It occurred to him that in spite of his misgivings about traveling with a friendly grizzly bear, there was some reassurance in knowing that no one was going to sneak up on them—not as long as Ebenezer was prowling in the vicinity.

As was his habit, Gray Feather opened his book before the firelight prior to crawling into his blankets. To the dismay of the trappers bedding down, Ebenezer came lumbering through the campsite and immediately sat down beside Gray Feather. The shock of the big bear's unexpected visit drove the men to their shootingware again. Of all of them, Gray Feather was the most surprised.

Only Petey chortled happily. "Ebenezer wants ye to read to him again."

"You sure have a way with them bears," Archuleta said.

"It's that deep, manly voice," Meek put in.

"Too bad it doesn't have the same effect on the ladies!" Menard added.

Gray Feather peered over the book at him. "And what makes you think it doesn't?"

The men had some fun at Gray Feather's expense. But the Ute took it in easy stride, ignored their barbs, and began reading to the bear . . . and whoever else wanted to listen.

Chapter Seven

"Remember to keep to low land and take care not to skyline yourself, Joe."

Meek shoved a boot into the stirrup and swung up onto his horse. "You don't have to tell me that. I know how the stick floats, Kit."

"I know you do. That's why I'm sending you back. The truth is, I'd as soon have you at my side. But this is the way it's gotta be."

Meek nodded. "Blaze a trail I can easily follow, Kit, 'cause this child is coming back just as soon as I bring these coons to den."

They had built a travois for Overmier, who was suffering mightily from his wounds. Kit had cut the arrows from his flesh without much trouble, but fever had set in and already pus had begun to form. Kit worried that at any time that mysterious, malodorous greening of the skin might begin. If it did, Overmier would need more help than Kit or anyone else short of a real doctor could give. He hoped that Dr. Whitman was already at the rendezvous. If the arrows had been poisoned as Manhead suggested they might be, there would be little anyone could do for Overmier except wait for the end to come . . . an always painful, and oftentimes lengthy process.

The trappers saddled up and, after bidding a final farewell, Meek took the lead and started them south. Kit watched the men cut across the meadow to one side of the spouting fountain, which at the moment was merely steaming quietly between its regular eruptions. Meek led the party into the forest beyond the fountain and then they were gone.

"Time for us to be moving too," Kit said, taking up his reins and lifting himself onto the saddle.

The men saddled up.

Kit had already scouted out the Blackfeet's trail, and he set upon it at once. The Indians had made no attempt to hide their passing. They traveled as if they were certain no one would be following them. If nothing else, Kit had the element of surprise on his side. Ruefully, he had to admit that surprise alone would do very little to tip the odds, considering that the numbers were all stacked in the Blackfeet's favor.

Several times that morning Kit had stopped to scan the forest for signs of Ebenezer, but if the bear was sticking close to Petey, he had not shown himself.

"He's around" was the only comment Petey would give when Kit asked. Petey had grown sullen and aloof. Kit knew that the loner was still unhappy over his being in charge. But so far Petey made no move to test Kit's authority.

"They're not traveling fast," Gray Feather observed at one point as he and Kit pondered their tracks. The Blackfeet had left the protection of the trees here and had started across the grassy rise of a mountain slope.

"Have no reason to," Kit said. "They don't know we're trailing them yet, and even if they did, it would only give them Injuns delight to let us catch up with 'em. Never met a Blackfoot yet that didn't relish a fight just for the pure fun of it."

"How far ahead do you make it, Kit?" Menard asked.

"If they kept up their pace, I'd judge them to be a day ahead of us. If they made a camp, they could be anywhere. Over the next ridge even."

Manhead pointed to the grassy slope and said, "If they near, they know we are tailing them when we try to cross that."

"Manhead is right," Gray Feather said.

Kit knew it too. Once free of the forest, they could be seen for miles. "Unfortunately, we have no choice unless we want to make a wide loop to the south. That'll cost us an extra day."

"Can't afford to give 'em another day, hoss. Can't let them savages reach thar lodges. If they do, we can kiss them plews good-bye. Me an' Betsy say we push on and take our chances."

Kit swung a leg over his saddle and lighted upon the ground. "We'll wait here until dusk. They're leaving such a plain trail, we can follow 'em by starlight."

They made a small fire and boiled a pot of coffee. Petey paced impatiently, watching the sun lower in the sky. "We're wasting time here, hoss," he complained more than once.

"Bug's Boys will settle in for the night," Kit told him. "What time we've lost here we'll make up later. Instead of tromping around and working yourself up, you'd be better off catching some sleep or later you'll be napping in the saddle."

Petey hunkered down across the fire from Kit and glared at him with those bulging eyes. "Ye don't understand, hoss. Ye don't know the Blackfeet like I do. They're Ishmaelites clear to the bone, they are. They like nothing better than to make war, and they ain't happy 'less they're holding a weapon and planning some mischief!"

"I know the Blackfeet," Kit said. "It's true they relish making war more than a Rocky Mountain boy delights in kicking up his heels at a Taos fandango. And that's the reason I'm not gonna rush 'em now. Thar's only five of us, and maybe fifty or more of them. We can't fight 'em on thar own terms this time."

"Ye still don't understand, Carson. Those coons have stolen enough beaver to make them wealthy Injuns. And ye know what the Blackfeet do when they have gold in thar fists?"

"They go out and get drunk," Gray Feather said. "Kit and I had an encounter with a drunk Blackfoot war party down along the Missouri last spring, and I can tell you, they're worthless when they're drunk."

"Yeah, when thar drunk," Petey allowed. "But they buy not only whiskey but guns and powder, and when thar drunk wears off and thar heads stop a-pounding, they take thar new rifles and hit the warpath again. I tell you, blood will run deep in this country if them savages ever manage to get them pelts to market. Ye know that the Hudson's Bay Company does a right smart business in the Injun trade?"

"I intend to get those pelts back," Kit told him.

"You'll never get 'em back wastin' time here, hoss."

Menard said, "And we won't get them back if we run headlong into a Blackfoot war party who knows we're coming for them, either."

Manhead said, "Kit knows what he does. Him right. We need to rest now. Long ride tonight."

A little before sunset, Ebenezer showed up and startled everyone. The trappers just could not get used to the idea of a grizzly bear wandering freely through the camp. Petey seemed to relax after the bear's arrival and began talking to the bear, his rifle, and himself. They had themselves a lively conversation, at least as far as Petey was concerned. When it was finished, Ebenezer ignored the other trappers and sat in front of Gray Feather and just looked at him.

"I'm not in a reading mood right now, Ebenezer," Gray Feather told the bear.

The grizzly shook its huge head and remained there, staring at Gray Feather.

"I thought you said he didn't like Indians," Gray Feather said, a hint of annoyance in his voice.

"He appears to like ye right fine," Petey said, chuckling. The loner's mood had improved some after his short talk with his two best friends.

Kit studied the bear with some misgiving. Ebenezer was docile enough when among them, which was a mighty unnatural thing in itself, but that wasn't what was worrying Kit. He didn't know what was. Ebenezer had never gotten in their way, and kept pretty much to himself, except for the few times he would wander into camp and give each of them a sniff, as if simply reassuring himself that he knew and recognized each and every man there. Kit could not put a finger on it. But he did know one thing: His mind would rest a lot easier if the bear was not tagging along with them now.

As soon as the sun set the trappers were on the move again. Kit had no trouble reading the signs left by the large war party. The nearly full moon rose among the smaller lights of the stars to clearly show the way. They had passed from the region of the steaming vents and had left the bubbling mud lakes behind. The Blackfeet were heading straight north, making for their lodges, which ranged along the headwaters of the Missouri River. Once in a while Kit would catch a glimpse of movement far off across the wide plain they were traversing. He suspected it was only Ebenezer, keeping pace at a distance as was his habit.

Sometime around midnight the Blackfeet's trail curved to the west and left the plains, entering thick timber again. Here the moon could not shine and the tracking became more difficult. Finally, after pushing on for another hour, Kit brought the party to a halt. They would have to wait for the morning light to continue their march.

The trappers were too exhausted to build a fire, and, curling up inside their blankets, were immediately asleep.

Morning came too soon. The weary men rolled out of their warm blankets to discover that a crisp frost had whitened the land. Jerked venison and coffee made for a hasty breakfast, and once again they were on the move.

In the daylight the trace was clear enough. It was a simple thing for Kit to follow. The Blackfeet had ridden single file through the forest, cutting a deep track into the soft, pine-needle carpet that lay beneath the trees.

Near noon the trappers entered a clearing surrounded by aspen trees and the character of the tracks changed. Kit dismounted and studied the crushed grass. The Blackfeet had stopped here and had built fires.

"Looks like this is where Bug's Boys made camp last night," Kit told the others. He surveyed the trampled ground, noting the many places where men had slept, and the hastily built brush corral where the horses had been kept. They had made four fires. The ashes of one of them was still warm.

Manhead studied the sleeping places and came back frowning. "I count forty-seven, Kit," he said. "That not include the night watch over the horses. Maybe four or five more."

"Puts thar number at right around fifty. And they aren't far ahead of us, boys."

"Have you decided what we're going to do with these savages once we catch up with them, Kit?" Menard inquired. There was a note of teasing in his voice, which was Menard's way when a powerful worry was weighing heavy on his mind. Kit knew that Menard, like all the rest of them, was struggling against serious doubts.

Kit grinned and said, "Whal, since thar's only fifty or so of them I figured I'd just send you and Petey in to give them a good thrashing. No sense in all five of us working up a sweat, is thar?"

"Is that what ye figured, hoss?" Petey spat a stream of tobacco juice at the ground near the toe of his moccasin. He apparently did not appreciate the humor. "Whal, I don't know about ye coons, but if that's what it takes to get my plews and horses back, whal, I'm up to the job."

Kit said, "And you've got vinegar enough to do the job, Petey."

"Damn tootin', hoss."

"What *are* we going to do, Kit?" Gray Feather said. "You can make light of it here, but two or three hours from now, when we five are facing those fifty Blackfeet warriors, it would be kind of nice to have a plan."

"Don't have a plan, Gray Feather. At least, not yet I don't. A lot will depend on how we find the Blackfeet, and where we find 'em. It's plain as the nose on your face we can't take 'em head-on."

"We'll have to depend on stealth," Gray Feather noted.

"It might be that all we can do is steal back the plews they took and skedaddle. Maybe the best we can muster is to follow Bug's Boys and learn where they take 'em."

"We could wait until Meek returns," Menard said. "With half a hundred boys on our side, Bug's Boys will scatter to the winds. They do like a good fight, but they're sensible enough to know to turn tail and run when they're outgunned."

Kit nodded. "I've been thinking that too. Like I said, we're all just gonna have to wait and see how this hand plays out. If the opportunity comes for us to take back the plews and make good our getaway, then that's what we'll do. But on the other hand, if the best we can do is sit tight and wait for Meek and the others to show up . . . whal, we'll do what we have to."

"In other words, you *really* don't have a plan," Gray Feather said.

Kit grinned. "Looks like we've come full circle, heh?"

"Whal, while ye boys are standin' here jawing about it, Bug's Boys are getting farther away." Petey stepped into the stirrup and swung up onto his horse. "I'll be up ahead whenever ye coons decide to come along," he said, clucking his horse into motion.

"He sure is in a sweet mood," Menard said.

"And getting sweeter by the mile," Kit agreed, getting the party moving again.

* * *

Crouched on the brow of a hillside with their horses tethered below, Kit and the trappers looked down on the campsite that sprawled along a rushing stream. To his left the stream cut back between towering rocky cliffs, while in the other direction its fast waters tumbled through a forest of widely spaced pine trees. The Blackfeet were spread out beneath those trees, assembled in their clan circles, each around their own campfires.

The sight of such sheer numbers of hostile Indians was enough to make spines tingle and brows break out in beads of sweat. The coming evening chill didn't help matters any. Stationed at Kit's left, Gray Feather pointed across the campsite to a makeshift corral of rope strung between five or six trees and whispered, "There are the packhorses they stole, Kit."

Kit frowned. The Blackfeet had chosen a perfect place to stop. There was no easy way to enter their camp without being spotted. To his left, the steep mountainside blocked that avenue. To his right, the rushing water made it impossible to steal across to the horses unseen. "Almost looks like they were expecting us," Kit said finally.

"Those horses might just as well be in Missouri," Menard commented softly at Kit's right.

"What do you think, Kit?" Gray Feather said.

Shadows had begun to gather beneath the trees. Dusk was nearing, but for the moment there was still enough light for Kit to peg every detail of the camp below and commit them to memory. If he had to enter among the sleeping Blackfeet sometime during the night, he intended to know exactly where everything was.

Kit said, "They're keeping those horses mighty close, Gray Feather."

"Too close for us to steal them away during the

night without waking that whole camp, you think?"

"If it was only the horses we wanted back, I might give it a try. But thar are all those plews, too." Kit pointed out the mound of beaver skins that the Indians had removed from the packhorses. "With over a ton of beaver to move, thar's no way the five of us are going to make away with 'em without waking up the whole camp and bringing Bug's Boys raining down on us—at least not here. Maybe thar next camp'll give us a better shot at the pelts."

"You think we ought to wait another day?"

"Don't see as we have a whole lot of choice, Gray Feather."

Petey crawled over. "Whal, what are we waiting for, hoss?"

Kit looked at him. "You got a plan in mind, Petey? Or are you just anxious to lose you hair today?"

"Dadgumit, hoss, all our things are right down thar, within spittin' distance. We gotta do something!"

Gray Feather said softly, "Give every man thine ear but few thy voice. Take each man's censure, but reserve thy judgment."

Kit, Menard, and Petey looked at Gray Feather. The Ute merely grinned and said, "*Hamlet,* act one, scene three."

"What the devil does that mean?" Petey demanded.

Kit said, "I think Gray Feather just warned you to keep quiet, Petey."

"He did?" Petey thought it over, scowling. Then he shook his head. "That Injun's just talking nonsense."

"Maybe," Kit said, "but most often his nonsense makes a lot of sense."

Movement down in the corral caught his eye. Concentrating on the animals now, he saw that a couple of the horses had begun to toss their heads and hold their noses high to the breeze. The animals pranced nervously and gathered together over on one side of the corral with their heads all facing the same direction. The two Blackfeet herdsmen had noted the peculiar behavior and were discussing it between themselves.

"Wonder what's going on down thar?" Kit said.

But Gray Feather had recognized the signs immediately. "Those horses have sensed something. They're nervous."

"Is it us?" Menard asked.

Manhead moved in closer. "No. See. The horses look away. To the east."

"What do you make of it, Gray Feather?" Kit asked. If there was any one man among them who had a special knack for handling and understanding horses, it was the Ute.

"Manhead is right. There's something to the east making those animals nervous."

As the trappers watched, the two Blackfeet who were watching the horses took up bows and arrows and stalked out of camp. As yet the rest of the warriors paid no particular attention to the activities of the animals or the herdsmen. Whatever was going on down there, it was still a matter for the few to take care of, not yet a concern for the many. As Kit watched, his brain ticked off a half-dozen possible scenarios. Each was a possibility, but none was likely until he happened upon one that brought his thoughts to a halt.

"Have any of you boys seen Ebenezer lately?" he asked. No sooner had he spoken than the bear's deep roar echoed up from the ravine below. Instantly the Indians scrambled to their feet and the camp became a beehive of motion as men reached for their weapons.

Petey's bulging eyes looked as if they were about to pop from his head. In the camp the Indians stood ready. The next moment one of the two herdsmen who had gone off came running back into camp shouting a warning, and right on his tail pounded the enormous grizzly bear. Ebenezer swiped out with one of his paws and laid open the man's back as neatly as if he were filleting a fish. The Blackfoot went down beneath Ebenezer's great bulk. Ebenezer took the man's head into his powerful jaws and clamped down on it, and with one powerful snap he tossed the man aside.

Turning suddenly, the bear charged into the main body of Indians. Petey watched in stunned silence, but when it became clear that the Blackfeet were about to impale his pet bear with a score of arrows, Petey gave out a startled cry.

"No you don't, you red sons of bitches!"

Before Kit could stop him, Petey shoved his rifle to his shoulder, took a bead on one of the warriors below, and touched the trigger.

Chapter Eight

Petey's rifle boomed. Down below a Blackfoot lurched headlong into the ground.

Their position revealed, Kit cursed the loner beneath his breath and lined up a Blackfoot in his sights. In near unison, the roar of the trappers' rifles crackled from the ridgeline and dropped a handful of Blackfoot warriors where they stood. Caught between the bear and an unknown number of whites above them, the Blackfeet hesitated an instant, not knowing which way to turn.

In that moment of indecision, Ebenezer plunged through their ranks, batting men aside as he strode into the fast stream and across. Above him, the trappers quickly reloaded and let loose with a second volley of gunfire. Hot lead mowed a wide row through the Blackfoot ranks.

Now the trappers had only moments to make good their own escape. Already the Blackfeet were scattering into the trees. Kit caught a glimpse of

Ebenezer climbing the slope, his huge muscles rippling the silver-tipped fur of his coat.

Kit scooted back from the ridge and said, "Let's get out of here!"

After scrambling down to where they had tied their horses, the men leaped to the saddle and buried their heels. Behind them came the war whoops of pursuing Indians. All at once a volley of arrows arched through the air, raining down upon the fleeing mountain men. Kit heard a dull thud nearby. Menard gave out a sudden groan and slumped in his saddle. His rifle slipped from his fist, but he managed to hold on to his reins, clutching a fistful of mane as he fought to stay in the saddle.

Kit yanked out a pistol and swung around, firing into the Indians scrambling over the valley's edge. Then the forest closed in and the Blackfoot arrows could no longer reach them. It would take many minutes for the Indians to regroup and ready their horses, minutes that Kit intended to use to put as much distance between them and Bug's Boys as possible.

Gray Feather had moved out ahead, his stout Indian pony leading the way, dodging through the close branches, leaping deadfalls, moving like the wind through the trees. Petey was right behind him, leaning low to his horse, hair flying as if he were riding a wild tornado. Kit slowed to keep pace with Menard. Manhead held to the rear, his practiced eyes keeping tabs on their back trail.

Menard was having a hard time remaining in his saddle. An arrow had entered his back up high and to the right of his spine. Kit feared it had punctured a lung. He saw the trapper's labored breathing.

"Just hold tight, Antoine," Kit said, taking the wounded man's reins. Menard slumped farther forward, keeping himself in place by sheer will and a firm grip on his saddle. Slowed down by the wounded man, Kit could not travel as fast as Gray Feather and Petey, and in a few minutes they had disappeared ahead. Kit kept the wounded man moving until he had put several miles between them and the Blackfoot encampment.

With the approaching night, traveling became even more difficult. Manhead rode up alongside Kit and said, "I don't think Blackfeet will follow in the night. They have many dead and wounded to tend to."

"We need to find someplace where we can take that arrow out of Menard's hide."

Manhead shook his head slowly. "Wound is bad one. Taking out might make worse."

Menard turned his head, pain pulling his face into a mask of agony. Through his suffering he managed to say, "Just leave me, Kit. Save yourselves. I'm done for anyway."

"I'm not gonna leave you, Antoine. Don't talk. Save your strength."

He gave a short laugh. "Ain't . . . ain't got none to save, Kit," and with that Antoine Menard passed out.

Manhead reached out in time to catch the trapper by the sleeve before he slipped from his saddle. Kit brought the horses to a stop. They lifted the wounded man from the saddle and laid him on the ground. Kit sliced open the buckskin shirt. The arrow had gone deep. Manhead was frowning. The blood foamed from around the shaft in a bright crimson froth with each labored breath. As Kit had feared, a lung had been punctured.

"Help me move him, Manhead."

The two men carried Menard deeper into the forest, away from the horses. In the protection of a rock outcropping, they laid him in the deepening shadows. Kit prepared wood for a fire, poured a measure of black powder onto it, and struck a spark from his tinder box. As the small flame grew, Gray Feather and Petey suddenly appeared from the gathering gloom.

"I suspected some trouble when I looked back and you and the others weren't there," Gray Feather said. He dismounted and hunkered down by the fire, his eyes studying Menard. "Circled back and found your horses. You left a trail a blind man could follow."

" 'Fraid that couldn't be helped."

"How bad is it?"

"He took it in the lung. Collapsed it, I think. Trouble breathing. I'm not a doctor enough to cut it out without doing Menard more hurt than good."

"My experience in such matters is ye're better off letting the arrow alone for the time being," said Petey. "If he's lucky, the bleeding will stop on its own. He still has one good lung to keep him going. Ye go to cutting on a thing like that, not knowing what ye are doing, ye'll send him on to Glory for a certain."

For once Kit could agree with Petey. He ringed the shaft of the arrow with his knife and carefully snapped it off, leaving an inch still protruding.

Manhead found a stream nearby and came back with a canteen of water for Menard.

Kit said to Manhead, "Ride down our back trail and keep an eye open for them Blackfeet."

"Right."

"I'll ride with ye," Petey told the Delaware.

The two men drifted into the night as silently as a cloud of smoke.

Menard groaned, and in his unconsciousness tried to roll onto his back. Gray Feather stopped him. "We've got ourselves in the frying pan this time," he said as Kit rolled a blanket and wedged it behind the wounded man. Gray Feather fixed a poultice and packed it around the shaft.

"He's in a real bad way, Kit."

"It wouldn't be so if that b'ar hadn't raged through thar camp like he did."

"Least we know Petey was telling the truth when he said that Ebenezer hated Indians, and Blackfeet in particular. Wonder where he is now."

"Far away from here, I hope."

"You don't think they managed to kill him, do you?" Gray Feather said, suddenly worried.

Kit looked over, surprised. "To hear you talk it sounds like you've developed an affection for that white-tipped monster."

Gray Feather grinned. "He appreciates literature . . . unlike some humans with whom I'm acquainted."

Kit shook his head. "Just goes to show it sure don't take much to win some folks over."

Neither man was inclined to sleep that night. They took turns, one keeping an eye on Menard while the other hunkered in the shadows among the rocks where he had a clear shot at their campsite, in the event that any Blackfoot might care to pay a visit. The night seemed to go on forever. Finally Kit was encouraged by the faint tinge of pink spreading across the eastern sky. The far-off hoot of an owl that had serenaded them all night diminished, replaced now by the twittering of smaller birds out to catch that early worm.

A herd of elk appeared in the misty light not far off among the trees. They drew up, startled to discover humans in what Kit surmised to be their regular path down to the stream where Manhead had collected water the evening before. Men and beasts stared at each other for a long while, beast not sure what to make of these intruders, and man thinking that a rump of elk would make for a mighty fine breakfast. But Kit resisted the urge. If the Blackfeet were out and about, searching for them, a rifle shot echoing though the forest would bring them running. In the end, the elk drifted off to the south of the trappers and melted back into the deep shadows that still clung to the ground beneath the trees.

Kit spied movement from another direction. He took up his rifle, but it was only Gray Feather coming in from a wide loop around their camp.

"No sign of them at all, Kit. They must have figured we were too much for them to handle."

"I wouldn't write Bug's Boys off that easily, pard. Thar not a forgiving sort. We bloodied thar nose some last evening, and now they have wounded to care for. But I expect they've already sent bucks to sniff out our trail. It's just a matter of time before they find us."

"Wonder where Manhead is. He's been out all night."

"He's got mountain savvy. He'll be all right." Kit frowned. "But I'm not so sure about Petey."

"Petey has survived out here for three years all by himself. You don't do that without some mountain savvy, Kit."

"He might have the savvy," Kit allowed, "but all that lonesome living has màde him sorta weak north of his ears."

Gray Feather laughed. "He just needs to be around his own kind for a little while. Why, I've seen improvements in him already."

"Oh? What kind of improvements?"

Gray Feather had to think hard on that one a while. "Well, for one thing, he isn't talking to that rifle of his as frequently as when we first ran into him."

"Whal, maybe ol' Betsy is upset with him joining up with us."

Gray Feather gave a short laugh and went back to guarding their camp. Manhead and Petey returned shortly afterward. Kit had boiled a pot of coffee over the small fire, and after each man had taken a cup of it, Manhead told Kit what had transpired that night.

"We found no one on our trail, Kit. Petey and me follow it back to the Blackfoot camp. Much going on. Much war drums most of night. We crawl in real close. In firelight I count eight dead, another four with wounds."

"We done it to 'em real good," Petey said, swinging a fist through the air. He cackled. "Shot 'em in the lights, we done. Showed them Injuns we white men got the ha'r of the b'ar." He patted his rifle affectionately. "Betsy here brought two of 'em coons to beaver."

Kit said, "The only reason we got out of thar with our scalp still attached was because we took them by surprise."

"Ye can thank Ebenezer for that, Carson."

"Thank him? That b'ar nearly cost us our lives. Might have already cost Menard his."

"How is he?" Manhead asked.

"In a bad way," Kit said. "I tried to make him comfortable through the night and give him drink, but that arrow is gonna have to come out soon if he's gonna have any chance at all. Gray Feather fixed a poultice. Bleeding appears to have stopped. Breathing's coming hard, though." Kit glanced at Petey. "It's because of that b'ar of yours that he's in such a fix."

Petey looked around. "Speaking of Ebenezer, anyone seen him about?"

"No," Kit said flatly.

Petey looked worried.

Manhead continued with his story. "We stay near their camp until dawn. I want to see if they pull out and go north, to lodges. They not. It look like they make ready for war, prepare to follow our tracks. We leave in big hurry. Want to make it back here and warn you."

Gray Feather was already working out the odds. "Twelve down leaves thirty-eight to forty left. They won't all come after us at once, some will have to stay behind to tend the wounded and guard their horses and pelts. They still don't know how many we were, so they'll send as many men as they can afford."

Kit said, "Once on our trail they'll figure out real quick that we're only a handful."

Gray Feather went on. "Let's say ten remain behind to watch their camp. That leaves maybe thirty to come looking for us."

Manhead grunted. "Thirty against four. I no like those odds, Gray Feather."

"They do seem rather lopsided. But they are improving," Gray Feather added encouragingly.

"Improving?" Petey hooted. "If them savages ketch up with us we'll have as much chance as a grasshopper in an anthill!"

Kit said, "Unfortunately, Petey's right, boys."

"What do you propose we do?" Gray Feather asked.

Kit looked at Menard. "It's for certain we can't go moving him very far by horseback, and a travois would leave a trail a blind Injun could follow."

"Sounds like we're facing the same problem we done with Overmier," Petey groused.

Kit had suspected that the Blackfeet would come looking for them and he had already considered and discarded several plans. But one had stuck in his head as having possibilities, and it was this one he laid out before them now.

"If we can't move Menard without killing him, then maybe we can move our trail."

Manhead lifted an eyebrow and said, "Put down a false trace for them to follow?"

"That's what I'm thinking."

"How?" Gray Feather asked.

"The way I figure it, we can make up a litter out of a couple poles and our blankets. Taking care not to leave spoor for Bug's Boys to follow, two men could carry Menard a good distance along this rocky ground. They might easily make a mile or so, then set up a new camp."

"And by the way, what would the other two men be doing, hoss?" Petey asked.

"First off, they'd linger here long enough to make sure no tracks were left behind. The Injuns will surely find this place and see that we spent the night here. If they think we left, the natural thing for them to do is follow. We'd take the horses with us so they'd have no reason to suspect that we split up. We'll run them on a merry chase, and once they've lost our scent, we'll circle back and rejoin."

Petey was frowning.

Manhead considered the plan and slowly nodded his head. "It can work."

They heard the sound of movement out in the forest. The trappers had already learned to recognize Ebenezer's shambling gait, and the snapping twigs beneath his weight. His arrival this time did not startle them as it had in the past. The bear appeared in the distant gloom of shadows that still hugged the earth.

Petey gave a shout of delight and waved an arm at the bear. "Ye finally found us, ye lughead."

The bear did not come rushing into camp as had

been his habit, but slowed and finally stopped a few dozen yards out. He stood there watching, as if now he wasn't sure of them.

"What's got into ye—" Petey began, then stopped. He advanced a few steps, eyes large. "Great Glory, Ebenezer, them Injuns went and put an arrow in ye!" Petey rushed to the bear, who only tentatively allowed the man who had been his friend since he was a cub approach him. Coaxing him with soothing words, Petey brought the silver-tipped monster into camp. A Blackfoot arrow had embedded itself in the bear's left rear haunch. "Ye went and got yourself shot again," Petey declared. When he tried to examine the wound, Ebenezer roared and sidestepped out of reach. The grizzly retreated even farther when Kit and Gray Feather tried to approach him.

"Now, ye just settle down, Ebenezer," Petey cooed, running a hand gently along the mountain of fur. "We're gonna have to cut that arrow out of ye." Speaking gently, Petey gradually regained the confidence of the bear. Slowly Ebenezer settled down. But when Petey worked his hand back toward the arrow, the bear shied away.

"Worse than a blushing bride on her wedding night," Petey scolded the bear. "Now let me take a gander at that wound. I'm only tryin' to help ye!"

Gray Feather said, "Let me try something."

"Ye? Shoot, hoss, if ol' Ebenezer don't trust me, he sure ain't gonna trust nobody else—'specially someone with the smell of Injun about him!"

In a calm, sure voice, Gray Feather began reciting a scene from the *Merchant of Venice,* the one where Antonio asks the moneylender, Shylock, for a loan for his friend, Bassanio. By the time Gray Feather got to the place where Shylock berates Antonio for the shabby treatment he and his people had received, the bear had settled down and was listening with rapt attention. He gave a low growl and sat down on his right hip. He allowed Kit to approach, he permitted Petey to touch the arrow, and he gave hardly a cry when Kit's sharp knife pried it from his thick hide.

Petey shook his head and declared he'd never seen anything like it. Gray Feather continued with his recitation to the end of the scene, after which Ebenezer stood, favoring his left hip, and sniffed the air, becoming excited when he neared Menard and smelled blood.

"You leave him be," Petey admonished the bear, and shooed him away.

The trappers constructed a crude but effective stretcher out of young aspen trees and blankets. The dawn was full in the sky now, morning sunlight eating away at the misty shadows. Kit was anxious to be on the move, for he was certain that by now the Blackfeet were hounding their trail.

"Manhead and Petey will carry Menard away from here. Gray Feather and me will see that your tracks are brushed away. I reckon if you head due east and put maybe two miles' distance from this place, we'll be able to find you easy enough once we throw them Injuns off our trail."

"Wait a minute, hoss. I'm not gonna go off and hide and let ye two have all the fun."

"This ain't for pleasure, Petey, and you *will* go with Manhead."

"Will not."

"Where you go, that b'ar goes, and he already cost us one wounded man, busting up that Blackfoot camp like he done. I'll not have him following along now, not knowing from one minute to the next if he's about to give away our position to the Blackfeet."

"Ye ain't my booshway, Carson. I go whar I please."

In a heartbeat Kit drew his pistol and thumbed the hammer, leveling the piece between Petey's bulging eyes. "Normally I've got the patience of Job, Petey, but not today. You do as I say or by God when the Blackfeet find you thar won't be enough left of your head to scalp."

Petey's eyes nearly slammed together as they stared at the big bore of Kit's pistol. "Ye'll regret ye done this, Carson."

"Maybe. Maybe not. Reckon we'll just have to cross over that bridge when we come to it."

Chapter Nine

Kit and Gray Feather carefully swept away Manhead and Petey's tracks, then scattered the pine-needle litter across the places that had been trampled. Kit spent extra time eliminating all traces of Menard's blood from their campsite. When the Blackfeet got to this place, Kit did not want to reveal any more about the trapper's condition than was necessary. It was true that the Blackfeet would have determined their strength long before reaching this spot, but Kit saw no reason to advertise to them that at least one of the men had been wounded.

There was little Kit could do to eliminate the signs that a huge grizzly bear had been in the vicinity, and he did not even try. If the Indians did make the connection between the bear and the trappers at all, the very presence of Ebenezer with the mountain men would confound them and perhaps intimidate them. Bears held a place of almost mystical quality with most Indian tribes. Discovering that one of the great beasts was friendly to whites would be a powerful omen that no self-respecting Blackfoot could completely ignore.

When the Crows had discovered Petey and Ebenezer together, they left the pair strictly alone. Kit did not know how the Blackfeet would see the matter, but he hoped their reaction would be similar.

"That about does it," Gray Feather said, bringing the horses forward. They had been careful to leave the footprints in their camp undisturbed. Kit did not want the Blackfeet to suspect that any effort had been made to conceal their activities.

"Reckon if we're lucky, Bug's Boys won't look too closely at what we done here and stay on our trail."

The Ute nodded. "They have no reason to suspect that we didn't all ride out together."

"Even so, a sharp tracker will see that it's so." Kit knew that a careful tracker would notice that several of the horses now carried no riders, whereas before they had. The almost insignificant difference in a hoofprint would escape the casual eye, but it would be plain enough to a seasoned scout. A skilled tracker himself, Kit was always on the lookout for the small details that told the true story, details such as the way a horse placed its hoof when burdened or unburdened. But as Gray Feather had said, the Blackfeet had no reason to suspect a dodge, and perhaps these faint signs would escape them now.

Gray Feather had put the extra horses on long leads to give the appearance that they were each being ridden separately. Kit tied the pine boughs used to brush away the tracks onto the saddle of one of the riderless horses. If he had left them behind and they had been found, the Blackfeet would have known at once what had happened.

Kit swung up onto his saddle, and casting a look over his shoulder at their handiwork, he said, "Now, let's give them Injuns something to follow."

Kit led one of the horses while Gray Feather, following behind him, led the other two. They rode swiftly, keeping clear of the thick timber, preferring to follow the grassy valleys and meadows where they could make better time while leaving a clear trace for the Blackfeet to follow. At least, Kit mused, he did not have to worry about Ebenezer showing up. The bear had disappeared shortly before Manhead and Petey had left carrying Menard on the stretcher. Kit was certain that at this moment the bear was following the strange, wild-eyed loner, thankfully miles away.

Gray Feather said, "I've never seen you point a gun without intending to use it, Kit. Would you have carried out your threat?"

It was a question to which Kit did not have an answer. At the time it seemed the simplest way to end Petey's rebellion. It was not as if they had all day to discuss the matter, not with Indians closing in on them. "I don't know, Gray Feather. I'd not like to think I would have, but we were running a mite short on time, and I was plum out of patience with that coot."

"Well, standing him down like that did not sweeten his disposition any."

Kit gave a short laugh. "A whole hogshead of molasses wouldn't be enough to sweeten Petey's disposition any."

Gray Feather grinned and went back to watching for the Blackfeet.

Like Gray Feather, Kit's eyes were in constant motion, his ears straining for the small, often missed sounds that signaled a looming attack. But so far he had not seen hide nor hair of the enemy that he knew must not be far behind them. And that made his skin crawl.

Kit was getting a mite skittish now.

"For forty years now I ain't never let no man tell me whar I can go and whar I can't!" Petey glanced at his rifle, which was presently riding upon the stretcher beside Menard. "Ain't that right, Betsy? Why, if only I had but a moment to grab ye up, or my knife or tomahawk . . ." Petey chuckled. "That coon would be whistling a different tune, he would."

Petey stumbled on the rocky slope, caught himself, and glared at Manhead, who was in the lead. "Slow up thar, ye long-legged galoot. I'm liable to drop my end of this here litter." He'd been scrambling for most of fifteen minutes to keep up with Manhead's long, sure strides. Not that Petey couldn't hold his own against most men when it came to covering ground in a hurry. His long legs were a testament to that. But Petey was feeling testy over being ordered by Kit, and he wanted Manhead to know it.

But Manhead apparently did not hear Petey's demand, for he kept right along at his pace, even picking it up some. The Delaware had purposely chosen this particularly treacherous track across a barren rock surface to hide their trail.

Petey scrambled to keep up with the Indian. "Don't blame me if I drop this coon," he groused.

Upon the stretcher, lying on his stomach, Menard had regained consciousness and was gripping the poles on each side. "I'd not like to be dropped, Petey," he said, grimacing as each jarring step they took seemed to shoot bolts of pain through his body.

"Whal, I ain't no mountain goat!" Petey cussed

out a string of blue smoke and ended with "I'm fit to be boiled down for glue over Carson takin' my horse. Now I'm doing the work of a horse while he's off playing follow the leader with Bug's Boys."

As they scurried along the rock face, Petey caught a glimpse of Ebenezer a hundred yards or so in the forest. The bear trotted along in view for a few minutes, then disappeared again, and Petey redirected his eyes ahead, puffing as he hurried along. His arms and fists had begun to sting from the strain of hauling the wounded man up the steep incline.

"How long . . . ye intend . . . to keep this up, hoss?" he demanded between breaths.

But Manhead remained mute.

"Dadgum ye, Injun! Answer me . . . or I drop him here and now."

"Drop him and I take your scalp, white man."

"Ye and what other tribe, Injun?"

Manhead stopped so suddenly that Petey almost lost the poles. Menard groaned at the sudden jolt. "My grandmother could lift your hair with one hand, *white man*!"

The two men glared at each other.

"Seems to me it war ye grandmothers and great-grandmothers who lost all your lands to the Dutch and English a hundred years ago."

"Will you two quit growling at each other and get me someplace where I can lay still and die in peace?"

Petey considered dropping the stretcher and grabbing for Betsy to end this dispute, and he knew that Manhead was thinking the same thing. Well, if nothing else, he would stare the Injun to death! But just then Manhead broke off the contest and peered out across the top of the forest that lay beneath the rocky slope where they were standing.

His eyes suddenly narrowed, intent upon something that had caught his attention in the distance.

"Down, quick!" the Delaware said.

Petey was in no mood to take orders from anyone, but the sudden urgency in Manhead's voice was a surefire antidote for Petey's vexation.

"What is it?" Petey asked, grabbing Betsy off the stretcher and crouching behind a nearby boulder beside the Delaware.

Manhead pointed. Petey's bulging eyes followed the finger. The trappers had climbed three or four hundred feet in the mile or so since leaving the campsite, and from here they had a wide view of the forest. Petey glimpsed the place they had abandoned an hour earlier. Just beyond it he saw riders dismounting. There had to have been twenty or thirty. The distance was far too great to make an accurate count.

"Bug's Boys." Petey whispered the words even though the Blackfeet were much too far away to have heard him. He shaded his eyes against the morning sunlight and squinted. The distant shapes still remained slightly out of focus for Petey's eyes. "Your peepers are a mite younger than mine. What are they doing now?"

"They find the camp. Sneak in to take it."

"They're in for a surprise when they discover we've left them high and dry."

Manhead nodded. "Only hope Kit and Gray Feather wiped away our tracks good enough."

Although the intervening trees obscured much of what was happening below, and distance blurred his vision, Petey had no difficulty seeing the stealth with which the Blackfeet had spread apart into a large circle and were approaching the camp, closing in like a noose tightening around a felon's neck.

"They've figured out exactly whar we spent the night," Petey said, still whispering.

"They smell fire."

"Carson put the fire out. I seen him pour water over it."

"Old fire, wet ashes, are clear signs to the nose of a good tracker."

"Hmm. Whal, I sure hope them trackers ain't good enough to see through our little trick."

Manhead looked over. "You were the one who did not want to miss the fighting?"

"Shoot, hoss. I still don't want to miss out on the fun! It's just that I favor getting Menard to someplace safe and sound before I go off in search of it. If Bug's Boys somehow manage to sniff out our trail, Menard's a goner for sure. Ye and me, we can fend for ourselves right 'nough. This child has danced around bloodthirsty savages afore. But Menard thar, he wouldn't have a prayer in his condition."

Petey had lost sight of most of the Indians, but the little clearing where they had spent the night was still visible, and all at once a dozen or more Indians swarmed into it. Upon discovering the camp abandoned, they sniffed around, their weapons ready, until they were certain that the trappers were not about to spring an ambush on them. Petey could just make out one of the Indians waving his bow high overhead, and the next moment the little clearing filled up with the Indians who had stayed back in reserve, in case their extra numbers were needed.

"They look mighty disappointed, don't they, hoss?"

"Now they scout the trail," Manhead said.

The two trappers watched for a full five minutes

as the Indians mulled about their abandoned campsite below.

"They's sure taking their sweet time about moving on, ain't they?"

"Scout camp first."

"Think they smell a dodge?"

Manhead shook his head. "Too far away to see. They go in many directions scouting tracks."

"Sure hope Carson done a good job of hiding ours."

Petey and Manhead waited in cover, watching. It seemed to Petey as if the Blackfeet would never give up on the camp and move on. Then all at once the war party melted back into the trees and a moment later Petey got a glimpse of riders on horseback, starting on the trail Kit had laid down for them.

"Took the bait, they did." Then Petey squinted hard. "You see that, Manhead?" he said, pointing at what looked like a string of packhorses taking up the rear of the column.

"I see. They have pelts with them."

"Gray Feather figured they'd leave 'em behind with the wounded. Looks like they had other ideas." Petey glanced over and saw that concern had darkened the Delaware's face. "What's ye thinking, hoss?"

"They not go home to lodges."

"It don't look like it."

"They go on." Manhead frowned. "Why?"

Petey shook his head. It didn't add up in his brain either. "They don't want to take the pelts home with 'em. But someplace else."

The two picked up the wounded man and continued up the rocky slope. At the top, Manhead cut straight into the forest. With the Blackfeet already diverted off their trail, it seemed a waste of effort to hide their tracks, and Kit would need to have some sign to follow if he was to ever find where they had stopped to wait.

With trees close in about them they stopped in a damp hollow near a trickle of water, cool and fresh with the spring snow melt in the higher elevations. They made Menard as comfortable as possible. Menard had begun to run a fever. Manhead cooled his brow and neck with a cloth soaked in the cold stream.

Petey built a small fire beneath an overhang of rock. He scraped the dry heartwood from a rotting tree so that the fire would not smoke. There was plenty of deadfalls for good, dry wood and the fire burned hot. The small tendril of smoke it gave off dissipated by the time it reached the middle branches overhead. They carried a coffeepot with them and some supplies, including a little coffee. Petey angled a stick over the small flames and started heating their water.

"I reckon ye're all set here, Menard," Petey told the wounded man as he and Manhead ate a lunch of hot coffee and hard, dried venison. Manhead intended to hunt some fresh meat later, after he had scouted the area. But he planned on doing his hunting far away from it, just in case his shot was heard by unfriendly ears.

"By the signs, I'd judge thar be game a-plenty all around this little hollow. The water is cool and sweet. 'Nough firewood to carry a man clean through winter if need be. Yep, this place do shine. I'd say ye're sitting pretty here, Manhead." Petey glanced at his rifle leaning against the trunk of a tree. "What do ye say, Betsy? Betsy says ye two will fare better than a coyote on hump-ribs."

"What you talk about?"

Petey glanced at the tree where Manhead's rifle

rested, at the moment well out of his reach. Petey took a sip at his cup. "Good coffee. Sure beats roasted acorns."

Manhead sliced a piece of jerked meat with his knife and soaked it a moment in a bowl of water before pitching it into his mouth. "Better roots for coffee than acorn."

"Is thar, now? I wished I knowed of 'em. Wished I had ma a jug of good Keen-tucky whiskey, but Ebenezer went an' drunk it all up on me."

Manhead looked over, his dark eyes revealing nothing of what he was thinking.

"Yep, that b'ar sure do like his whiskey. Only, ye best be wide-eyed careful when he's had his fill of it, 'cause Ebenezer gets mighty wild when he's drunk. Like to have torn my camp completely to pieces after he finished my only jug. I didn't want him to have it, but once he found it thar be no taking it away from him."

Petey stood and set his cup upon a rock. Moving casually, he took up his rifle and checked the priming powder in its pan. He laid the rifle across his shoulder and said, "Whal, ye take good care of that coon. Keep him warm and watch that fever."

"What?"

Petey grinned. "Reckon this is where ye and me part company, Injun."

Manhead's eyes narrowed. "Where you going?"

Petey swung the rifle off his shoulder, leveling it at the Indian when he attempted to stand. He drew back the flint. "I'm going after them pelts. Reckon Menard don't need my help now, not with ye here."

"Kit want you to stay here. Wait for him to come."

"Whal, now I feel real bad about that," he said, stepping around the Indian and taking Manhead's rifle. Backing up and keeping the rifle pointed, Petey said, "I'll just take this here bull thrower with me to keep ye from getting any ideas about stopping me. Since I ain't the sort to let a man go unarmed in this country, I'll leave it for ye a little ways off. Reckon ye're a good enough tracker to find it after I'm gone. Don't try to follow me, Injun. I'm not easy to trail, and I'm a right decent shot. Anyway, Menard needs ye here."

Manhead did not try to stop Petey as the loner backed out of the camp.

Petey kept the Delaware in his sights until he'd gone a hundred yards. Then Petey wheeled around suddenly and was gone.

Chapter Ten

With the afternoon sun warming the back of his buckskin shirt, making him drowsy, Kit urged his horse up to the steep game trail. Finally, after what seemed to Kit—and his horse—an endless climb, the trace leveled off upon a wide ledge of land several acres across, heavily timbered, and looking out over the valley they had left behind by means of a dozen or more switchbacking trails.

Kit heard Gray Feather's stout Indian pony snort as the Ute reined it in alongside him.

"A body can see the whole of the valley from up here," Gray Feather remarked as both men sat there, giving their mounts a well-deserved rest.

Kit noted that the thick timber here was a natural blind to anyone scanning the ridge from below. The trail they were following continued on, climbing eventually to the mountain peaks he'd glimpsed in the distance a while back when it had swung past a gap in the trees. But from here, all he could see was the long valley below them and snatches of the trail on its far side where he and Gray Feather had ridden over an hour earlier.

For a moment the only sound Kit heard was the twittering of birds in the forest and the heavy breathing of their horses. They were reassuring sounds—especially the birds. Kit swung stiffly out of the saddle, wrapped his reins around a branch, and walked to the rim of the ledge. The timbered land beyond the toes of his moccasins angled steeply away to the valley floor. A fine silvery thread was strung along the bottom of the valley. Kit knew that in reality that thread was a good-size stream, for he and Gray Feather had splashed across it before starting this steep ascent.

Gray Feather found a convenient deadfall and sat down. He took a lump of dried venison from a parfleche, cut off a couple of slices, and offered one to Kit.

Kit sat next to his friend. "Right pleasant spot to rest," he said, gnawing at the tough meat. "No water, though. A man couldn't spend much time here."

"There will be water ahead," Gray Feather said.

The two men sat there for maybe five minutes without speaking. They just listened and watched—watched the trail across the valley. Each had already reasoned out that if the Blackfeet were indeed on their trail, at some point they would have to appear on that trace. As it stood now, neither Kit nor Gray Feather knew for certain that they *were* being followed.

Kit finally broke the pleasant silence. "Hope Manhead and Petey got Menard to safe ground."

Another few minutes of silence settled upon them.

"Menard's a tough bird," Gray Feather said, expressing the concern that was on Kit's mind.

Kit watched the distant stream, his eyes unblinking. Sunlight flashed hypnotically off its moving water as if from a thousand tiny moving mirrors. Neither of them had slept the night before, and now Kit was exhausted. This small respite in their effort to lead the Blackfeet away from their wounded companion was just what Kit needed now. A beam of sunlight found its way to the forest floor and shone upon his legs and hands, and the long J. J. Henry rifle resting there. Kit leaned back against the trunk of a tree and closed his eyes, feeling its warmth bathe his face and the short growth of whiskers upon his cheeks and chin. It had been over a month now since he'd taken a razor to them. He planned to take care of that oversight just as soon as they reached the rendezvous.

"Think we'll ever recover the stolen pelts, Kit?"

Gray Feather's question startled Kit. He opened his eyes and sat up, realizing that just that quickly he had dozed off . . . a dangerous thing to do in Blackfoot country.

"Reckon if Meek shows up like he promised, then we can go get back our property."

"Maybe. But if Bug's Boys reach their lodges before then, it will take more than fifty men to do the job."

What Gray Feather had said was true. Still, with Menard being badly wounded and there just being four who could shoot a gun, there was little else to do but to wait for Meek to return, and to try to keep far enough ahead of the Blackfeet to avoid having to fight them head-to-head.

Kit gnawed another piece of jerky. Gray Feather went to the horses for a canteen of water. When he returned Kit said, "Did you mean it back thar the other day when you offered to stake Petey to an outfit?"

"I meant it."

"Mighty generous of you, considering a coot like that's likely to up and disappear in these mountains and never show his face again."

Gray Feather patted the pouch of coins on his belt. "My money is just sitting here. I might as well put some of it to work for me. If he does run out on me, well, at least I know my money went to help someone. It's not doing anyone much good riding in my coin purse."

Kit laughed. "Now you're starting to sound like Charlie Bent. He thinks just like that. Always looking for some place to 'invest' his money." Kit shook his head, grinning. "Maybe that's why he's rich and all I own is this here rifle, my saddle, and what I can carry with me."

"If we do get our beaver back, you really ought to put some of the money away, Kit. You're a young man now, but twenty years from now you are not going to want to face these hardships anymore. You have your future to think about."

"Twenty years from now thar won't be any market for beaver," Kit said. "Demand for it is already beginning to dry up. Folks in Europe have decided they like thar hats made of silk instead of beaver."

"Styles change," Gray Feather agreed. "And that's even more reason why you should be thinking about your future, Kit."

"Whal, if the market dries up, I can always go to work for Charlie Bent. He needs meat hunters to keep his trading house stocked up. Already told me I could go to work for him."

They fell into another of their regular silences, but Kit was thinking about what Gray Feather had said. There was no denying that although the half-breed was a strange duck, he did have a streak of common sense running through him as wide as the old muddy Missouri. It was not as if Kit never pondered his future. He just didn't know where he wanted to spend it, or how. Living in the mountains like he did, the future was always a remote place, oftentimes not stretching out very far. In the daily struggle just to survive, it was today that most mountain men lived for, not tomorrow. For too many trappers, tomorrow never came.

"I've thought about that from time to time, Gray Feather."

"And what have you come up with?"

"Nothing yet. Not exactly, that is. I've considered buying myself a place down in Taos. I like the winters down south, and the people. I have me some friends living down thar."

"Charles Bent?"

"He's one of 'em. Thar's the Jaramillos too, and a few others."

"I think buying a house in Taos would be a smart way to spend some money."

"What about you?" Kit asked.

"Me? I'm not sure either."

"You've got an education. Thar's got to be more for you to do than risking your hide out here, trapping beaver for a few hundred dollars a year."

Gray Feather laughed. "There are other things. I've always wanted to be a teacher. You know that. It's why I came back here to my people. But Walkara didn't think his people needed to learn English."

"I know. He thinks someday everyone here will be talking Spanish."

"And maybe he's right."

"No telling what the future holds, I reckon. You can always go back east. Teach school in some fancy college. You're right smart enough for that."

Gray Feather frowned. "I don't think that will ever happen."

Kit heard the disappointment in his friend's voice, and he understood why. "Because you are Indian?"

"What white man would want to be taught by an Indian, even half of one?"

"They'd be a fool to pass over someone with your brains." But Kit knew it was true. Gray Feather would never be fully accepted in the white world, no matter how many years of college he had under his belt. "Thar are always Indian schools, aren't thar?"

"A few. I suppose I could get a job in one of them. The trouble is, the government wants Indians to be educated as whites, to remove the Indian from them. The Indians may wish to be instructed by me, but I doubt very much the government would approve of it."

Kit frowned. He was about to suggest that Gray Feather consider the Oregon territory where there was no government yet, but before he was able to say so, the trail far across the canyon suddenly filled with horses. Kit pointed, and the topic of their future was immediately forgotten. This very real threat may well end any dilemma they may be having about tomorrow.

"Well, that answers the question, doesn't it?"

"Reckon it does, Gray Feather."

As the Blackfeet passed across the small section of trail visible to the trappers high above, each man silently counted. When the last of the Indians had disappeared into the trees again, Kit said, "I got twenty-four."

"That's what I counted too. And did you see? They have the packhorses with them."

"Wonder why they didn't send them pelts on to their village with those who stayed behind?" Kit puzzled over that for a while, not reaching a conclusion.

"We going to wait here for them, Kit?"

The trapper grinned. "Not unless you want to bring that future you were just talking about to a real quick end."

"Not really. Who knows, maybe twenty years from now somebody might actually hire an old white-haired half-Ute-half-English professor of English literature."

"Reckon stranger things have happened."

They mounted up and rode away. The Blackfeet were still an hour behind them, but Kit and Gray Feather had lost their lead waiting for them to show up. At least now Kit knew which way the stick floated. He only wished he knew if Manhead, Menard, and Petey had gotten away safely.

"Come through here like a herd of buffalo, they did. Not a single care in the world, they got." Petey hunkered down over the tracks and sorted out their number. "Looks to me like thar are nigh onto two dozen or more, not countin' packhorses, of course. And making no effort to hide thar tracks at all. Hmm? What's that ye say, Betsy? Why, 'course they ain't expecting no one to be tagging along behind 'em." Petey cackled out loud to the clear noon sky and slapped his leg. "Whal, we'll show them savages a thing or two. Get our horses and plews back and have us some sport in the doin'!"

Petey began walking. His lean, wiry frame and long legs swiftly covering ground. He was mountain-hardened and had the endurance of a mule. But more than all that, he was alone again, and that was how Petey liked it. In spite of the loss of his animals and pelts, and with little concern over the prospects of being outnumbered twenty-four to one, Petey strode on, following the Blackfeet's trail in high spirits.

"Yep, get them plews back, then sell 'em off at Horse Creek . . . hmm? Whal, I don't know. Reckon I might go have me a look at that thar Oreegon place Meek told of."

Petey strode on. His brow suddenly furrowed and he glared sharply at the rifle resting in the crook of his left elbow. "I don't know about Bernice no more. Shoot, Betsy, I ain't seen her in five, six year. She likely takes me for dead by now. Probably took up already with that farrier what always come by the cabin to see to the horses." Petey's high spirits had suddenly sunk.

"What do ye mean?" he said after a moment. The thumb of his left hand gently stroked a dent in the rifle's stock behind the hammer spur. "Going back just to be sure she ain't got herself hitched again might be what some folks call decent, but it would make Oreegon that much further away. Shoot, Betsy, we're more 'an half the way thar right here where we stand." Petey became irritated. "Besides, what's all this talk about Bernice, anyway? Ye and me, we've done fine together. Bernice always did have a way about her, ye know that. Sort of a grating irritating manner, like a loose fiddle string. What should I go back to her now for?"

He walked on, his paces becoming more determined, heels slamming angrily into the forest floor.

"Don't want to talk about it no more," he blurted out a minute later, and swung the long rifle unceremoniously over his right shoulder.

Off to his right a mass of gray and brown fur lumbered into view. "Whal, ye finally showed up," Petey said when the bear trotted a wide circle around him and rose on his hind legs in the trail and gave a growl. He dropped back to all fours and followed along a few paces off to one side. "Ye fought shy of them strangers, didn't ye? All except that Injun, Gray Feather. Ye kinda took to him once he commenced to reading to ye from that thick book."

Petey chuckled.

"Whal, can't say as I blame ye, Ebenezer. This here territory is growing a mite too crowded for my liking. Once we get our plews and horses back we'll head west, how does that strike ye?

"Betsy and me was just talking about Oreegon territory. Sounds a right purty place, according to what that Meek fellow said, and thar ain't hardly but a handful of white people in it to get in our way—except for a few of them Tories. But we know how to handle Tories, don't we? Whupped 'em good back in '15. Do it again if need be."

Petey shot the bear a sharp look. "Don't ye go giving me grief about Bernice too." He softened his tone. "Whal, I just thought ye might be. Betsy is prodding me to go back and fetch that woman with us." His round eyes narrowed. "Don't tell me ye're siding in with her?"

He tramped on another dozen paces. "I don't want to talk about it now."

After another few steps he added quietly, "Probably already done gone and got herself hitched to that dadgum farrier anyway."

Glumly, Petey tramped on, losing himself in his thoughts, not paying particular attention to the plain trail he was following.

Chapter Eleven

Petey strode on all that afternoon, half thinking about the Blackfeet he was following, half thinking about Bernice, and generally arguing with Betsy and Ebenezer the whole way, although neither the rifle nor the bear seemed particularly offended by the loner's rantings. He'd made good time, had covered miles of forest, and was still trekking along sprightly when he tackled a singulary steep path up the side of a valley.

At its summit Petey had to stop. Puffing hard, he drew air into his burning lungs and ran a dry tongue over leathery lips. In spite of his hardened condition, the climb had been a killer. He bent over to catch his breath, then staggered to a deadfall to sit down. He wished now that he had taken a canteen along with him. At the very least, he chided himself, he should have slaked his thirst at the stream below.

"Whal, ye could have said something when we sloshed across it," he carped at Betsy.

From here he could see the long sweep of the valley, and the meandering stream with its cool water harkening. But Petey would be damned if he was going to tromp back down there just to have a sip of it. "We'll push on. Got to be water ahead, and we can't let Bug's Boys get us now, can we?"

Ebenezer was scouring the ground with his nose. He'd locked onto a scent that brought the bear to the very log Petey was sitting on. He examined it minutely and gave out a small growl that Petey knew meant excitement. The big silver-tipped bear sniffed his way back to the main trail, anxious to be on his way.

"Ye got yourself a snoutful of something? Is it thar scent? All right, I'm a-coming." Petey groaned softly as he stood and started on. This time the bear took the lead and held on to it, ranging always a hundred or more yards ahead of him.

"Push any harder, Joe, and you're liable to run us into the ground," Jim Bridger advised during one of their infrequent breaks.

Joe Meek was hunched over fresh tracks in the forest floor, frowning. "Already told you, Gabe. We've not a minute to lose. Kit and the others have themselves a passel of trouble on thar hands and we've already lost three days on them."

Bridger rocked back in his saddle and gravely nodded his head. He seldom smiled, being one of the most somber men in the mountain. That was why his friends tagged him with the sobriquet "Gabe," reckoning that the archangel by the same handle was a solemn creature himself.

"We'll find them, all right. But you won't do our

boys any favors bringing them up against all them Blackfeet if they're too tired to load a rifle." Bridger looked back at the party of mountain men, over a hundred mountain-savvy and wilderness-hardened Indian fighters.

When Meek had brought the word of Kit's dilemma, and of the butchering of Huntington and his men, he was instantly met with more volunteers than he had counted on. He'd hoped to round up fifty. Instead more than a hundred stepped forward, nearly a third of the men already gathered at this year's rendezvous. Meek had spent but five hours in camp.

Fortune had smiled on him, for it was during those five hours that Dr. Marcus Whitman and his party had shown up. Their timing could not have been better. They had been greeted with a mock Indian raid, which startled the women with them, and were immediately escorted to the rendezvous, where Whitman went to work doctoring Overmier's wounds. Then he and Meek and the rescue party were in the saddle. They had ridden all night to reach this place where Kit and Meek had parted ways only a few days earlier. Here Meek easily picked up Kit's trail.

But he was still two days behind him at the very least—more, if he took Bridger's advice and reined in his pace.

"Don't have time to rest, Gabe," Meek said.

"You rode all night and all day to reach Horse Creek, and now you've ridden another day and night back."

"I ride with my eyes open, Gabe, and sleep in the saddle. I'll ride a fortnight if need be. Gave Kit my word I'd be back." Meek grinned as he lifted himself back onto his saddle. "Besides, I don't want Kit to have all the fun whupping them red devils. These are thar tracks leading away. We're close now."

Bridger glanced at Dr. Whitman, the only man there not seasoned to mountain life. "How are you holding up, Doc?"

Dr. Marcus Whitman was a tall, quiet man with soft brown eyes and an even softer voice. But he was solidly built and tough as horseshoes, a friend of every man there. As an ordained minister of the Presbyterian Church, if he disapproved of the mountain men's drinking and swearing, and lascivious carousing with Indian women, he said nothing about it. In his own quiet and gentle way he tried to lead the men by his example. But these men of the Rocky Mountains were not his mission.

He'd come west the year before with his partner, the Reverend Samuel Parker, to minister to the Indians of Oregon. But Marcus Whitman had made it only as far as the rendezvous on the Green River. His arrival was a godsend to the many men needing the services of a *real* doctor. Among them was Jim Bridger. Whitman removed a three-inch Blackfoot arrowhead that had been buried in Bridger's back for over two years.

At the rendezvous' end Whitman did not continue on to Oregon with Parker, but decided instead to return to the States in the company of the St. Louis Company, to enlist recruits for the distant mission field. Parker had gone on to Oregon without him. Now Whitman had returned, as he had promised he would, and this time he brought his wife, Narcissa, with him—but more important to these men, he had brought his surgical knives as well.

"I'm holding up all right," he told Bridger. "If there are men out here in mortal danger, men who might need my service as a surgeon, then I say push on with all speed."

It was plain that Whitman was feeling the effects of their forced march, but he was determined to keep up.

Meek was pleased and proud of Whitman's spunk. He grinned at the doctor, gave him a wink, and started the men moving again.

Gray Feather was getting nervous. "How long are we going to keep on playing mice to those cats, Kit? It's coming to evening, and I'm not too thrilled over the prospect of making a camp with two dozen Blackfeet but a mile or two behind me. We escaped the Cheyenne once by the skin of our teeth, if you remember. This time I'd like to give ourselves more elbow room when we leave Bug's Boys sniffing a cold trail."

Kit had been working on a ploy to throw the Blackfeet off their trace and give them time to circle back and find Manhead and the others.

"Making camp sounds like a good plan to me."

Gray Feather stared at him.

"I'd say another hour should be just about right."

"It will be dark in another hour!" Gray Feather said.

"That it will. And I'd like nothing more than to build us a nice big campfire to keep the shadows at arm's length. How about you?"

"I'd like nothing better than to know what the devil you're up to."

"Just keep your eyes peeled for a stream. Reckon we should come across one soon enough."

"I hate it when you do this."

Kit smiled to himself as their horses followed a trail along the eastern flank of a narrow valley. It wasn't as if he was purposefully being evasive; it was just Kit's nature to ruminate upon a plan for a while, alone, turning the various problems over in his brain until it had grown some. Later he would present it to his partner and consider Gray Feather's suggestions. But for now, he just wanted to ponder it without distractions.

The valley forked and flowed into an adjoining basin about a mile ahead.

Gray Feather said, "Likely to be a stream or river up there, Kit."

Kit picked up their pace. He reckoned they were still an hour ahead of the Blackfeet, but because the scheme shaping up inside his head required a little time spent in preparation, he needed to widen that distance now.

A few minutes later Kit had put the finishing touches on his idea. He was ready to talk about it, and he asked Gray Feather, "If you were Bug's Boys, following a couple men who you figured didn't know you were behind 'em, what would you do come evening and you spied a fire up ahead?"

"I'd think the men I was following had stopped for the night. I'd think they had no idea they were being followed. Making a fire would be foolish otherwise."

"Especially a big one."

"You intend to draw them in?"

"Like moths. But first I want 'em to sit out a ways and think about it. Seeing our fire, they'd naturally figure they have us square in thar sights. Thar would be no need to hurry then."

"I think I understand."

"Eventually a scouting party would sneak in close, but by then we'd be long gone, and it would be too dark to follow our tracks—even if they could find them."

"You intend to lose them in the stream?" Gray Feather's voice held a note of skepticism.

"We got away with it once with the Flatheads, you remember."

"We were more lucky than two men had a right to be, and anyway, I was hurt too bad to advise you, if you remember."

Kit frowned, recalling their narrow escape from a village of supposedly peaceful Indians. Gray Feather had taken a musket ball in the side, and the way he had lain down a blood trail, Kit could only attribute their final escape to the hand of Providence.

"The stream bank would be the first place they'd look for our tracks come light."

"So what will you do, Kit?"

"We'll give 'em exactly what they expect . . . only not exactly."

"There you go. You're doing it again, Kit."

With the coming night darkening the sky, and the valley filling up with shadows, Kit found the stream he was looking for. He told Gray Feather to gather wood—lots of wood. "The greener the better," Kit said as he removed his buffalo coat from his saddle and began cutting large squares from the hide. It had been a good coat, nicely broken in, and had served him well through the winter. But the winter was past. Now it would serve again so that hopefully there would be more winters to come. He could barter for a new one at the rendezvous. The friendly tribes always showed up with trade goods to exchange for lead, powder, tobacco, iron arrowheads, pots, pans, and gewgaws for their womenfolk. Replacing the coat would be no problem.

Kit fingered the holes in its right sleeve, souvenirs of a battle he had had that winter with two ferocious dogs belonging to a band of Comanches. The battle had left the dogs dead and his right hand badly mauled. Even now, months later, there was still stiffness in it as he worked.

With fire steel and flint, Gray Feather struck a small, smoldering fire that he coaxed with his breath into a healthy flame.

"Build it up big," Kit told him as he hurried to complete his part of the job.

Gray Feather piled green pine boughs onto the flames.

As he had explained to Gray Feather earlier, he intended to lull the Blackfeet into thinking they had their quarry within easy reach. The big fire would tell the Indians that the trappers were unaware of their presence. By the time the Indians discovered the ruse, Kit hoped to be long gone. First, however, they would lay down a false trail.

"They will see this for miles," the Ute said, stepping back from the hot flames. "You about done?"

Kit had cut twenty squares of buffalo hide. "Nearly didn't have enough skin," he said, giving Gray Feather ten of the squares. Kit had had to cut up a pair of saddlebags to make the required number of thongs.

Before mounting up, they threw more wood onto the fire. Kit wanted the fire to burn for hours, and the heavy deadfall that they found and had dragged into the flames would ensure that it would do just that. Swinging back into their saddles, Kit and Gray Feather started off into the night. Kit took to the middle of the stream and started down it. After a few hundred yards, they turned the horses out of the water and started for a rocky wash that tumbled out of a side canyon, looking like a pile of bleached knucklebones in the pallid moonlight.

"This should do it," he said, swinging a leg over the saddle and dropping lightly to the ground. In the next few minutes the two trappers tied the buffalo skins to their horses' hooves, hair side out. Their hooves padded now to prevent leaving sharp tracks, Kit started them up the wash to throw the Blackfeet off. Then he turned back and guided the horses off the rocks, down again to the valley. They let go of the reins on the horses. Short of being spooked, the riderless animals would follow docilely along behind them, but spacing themselves in a natural manner that would eliminate the distinct trail they would make all bunched together.

Kit turned his horse back to the stream, reentering it this time several hundred feet above the place where they had built the huge fire that still shot tall flames into the night. The buffalo-hide hoof pads would make trailing a horse walking at an easy pace impossible at night, and difficult at best in the daylight. With no clear prints to follow, it would take even a superb tracker many hours to discover their trail back to the stream—and even more hours to identify the rocky cove in the bend of the stream where the riders had again emerged from the water. With all his backtracking and subterfuge, Kit figured that with any luck at all the ruse might never be discovered.

In any event, a mile or two of travel tonight followed by a cold camp and early departure in the morning practically assured them a trip back to Manhead and the others without the company of the Blackfeet.

Kit felt a wave of great relief as they started up a game trail in the dark, leading the three extra horses again. All he had to worry about now was getting Menard down out of these mountains and someplace where that arrow could be removed from his lung . . . or so he thought.

Chapter Twelve

All at once Kit drew rein.

"Now what?" Gray Feather whispered. "Blackfeet?"

But Kit had discovered no new danger. Instead he had realized that if they stole away into the night now, they would likely never get the pelts back. Kit looked back the way they had come, then glanced at his friend. He grinned at the puzzled look on Gray Feather's face. "Relax, pard. We're safe enough for the time being."

"Then why stop? Let's put some miles between us and those warriors!"

"If you were Bug's Boys, following a couple men who you suddenly discovered had given you the slip, what would you be thinking right now?"

"Kit," Gray Feather began impatiently, "we've already played this game—"

"Whal, let's play it again, coming at it from a different quarter this time. Let's say we were those

Blackfeet back thar. Say we sneaked into the trappers' camp where thar was a big fire burning and discovered that the trappers had given us the slip."

It was plain that Gray Feather would rather be riding away from here than playing these games with Kit, but he drew in a long, settling breath just the same and spoke with forced patience, almost as if appeasing the demands of a stubborn child.

"All right, let's say it's so. If I was one of those Blackfeet I'd probably figure—and rightly so—that the trappers had given me the slip and that they were better men than I. I'd then find someplace to get a good night's sleep and next morning return to my lodges and spin some heroic yarn about how my warrior friends and I chased the intruders from our land. I'd embellish it with enough half-truths so that it made for interesting telling around the campfires. I'd probably pass the story down to my children. If I could write, I would certainly record the deed, therefore assuring its place in history, regardless of how inaccurate the event really was. But then, accurate history would not be my motive. Saving face among the elders and the other warriors would be uppermost in my thoughts."

Gray Feather paused.

Kit sat there a moment, speechless. There was more depth to Gray Feather's answer than he had been looking for, and more truth there too.

"Shall I go on? I can, you know."

"No, you about covered it all."

"Did it help any?"

Kit nodded his head. "What I was looking for was that part about them Injuns spending the night."

"It would be the only choice left them now. They can't trail us in the dark—not after all the trouble we went through to hide our tracks."

"That's about how I see it," Kit said. "And what

better place to spend it than someplace where thar's a big fire already built for them, and water and grass nearby for thar horses."

"I still don't get what you are driving at, Kit."

Kit pointed into the night, more or less in the direction of the bonfire, which was now out of sight beyond an intervening ridge. "Bug's Boys will camp thar tonight. With 'em they have all our plews. Since we gave 'em the slip, they'd naturally be expectin' us to hightail it out of here just like you said. They run us off of thar land . . . or so they think."

Gray Feather caught Kit's drift. "That's right. The last thing they would expect is for us to turn back now." His enthusiasm died suddenly. "But what could just the two of us do, even if we do manage to sneak down there when everyone is asleep? We'll never get the packhorses away without waking the dead. And how far can we carry those heavy packs of beaver skins ourselves?"

Kit inclined his head at the three horses they were leading. "Got horses right here."

"They wear saddles, not pack frames," Gray Feather pointed out.

"Thar are pack frames below with the plews. We can leave the saddles if we have to. Buy new ones at the rend'vous with the money we get for the plews, and still be way ahead of the game. You're the one with a head for money, Gray Feather. You figure it out."

Reluctantly, the Ute nodded his head. "All right, that will solve the problem of hauling the plews. But we still have to steal them back again—from right under Bug's Boys' noses this time. How do you suggest we do that?"

"Don't know . . . yet," Kit said. "But we still have all night to work on a plan."

"We'll have to make our way out of there without

leaving a trail," Gray Feather reminded Kit.

Kit grinned. "I'm not hearing much enthusiasm in your voice."

"Well?"

"I already have that part of the problem figured out."

Exhausted, Kit and Gray Feather curled up in their blankets. The night had grown cold, but that was nothing new to the trappers. Even in the summer, nights spent in the Rocky Mountains were never very warm. In a few minutes both men were asleep. Kit's internal clock woke him sometime after midnight. Clouds of gray steam accompanied his breathing as he rolled out of the blanket and stood. He regretted not being able to light a fire to at least warm his hands by. Bitterly, he thought of Blackfeet enjoying the fire he and Gray Feather had built. He only hoped that by now its flames had burned down to coals and that the Indians were curled up in their own blankets, fast asleep.

"Time to go," Kit said, nudging his partner awake.

Gray Feather stirred and sat up. "What a time to wake me. I was having a wonderful dream," he murmured, rising stiffly, shivering.

Kit rubbed his hands together, working warmth into his stiff fingers. "What was it about?" He cupped his hands and breathed into them.

"I was maybe seven or eight years old, and back in my mother's lodge. There were warm bearskins on the floor, a fire burning, and I was bundled up in a rabbit-skin blanket. She was roasting elk over the fire and singing a song I haven't heard or thought of in almost twenty years." Gray Feather smiled at a sudden thought. "And my father was there too. My mother and my father were together again. She was wearing a soft, white doeskin dress, and he was in his best suit, his Sunday suit, with a heavy gold belly chain and a tall, silk hat on his head."

"Silk?"

Gray Feather frowned. "Well, maybe it was beaver. It was only a dream, after all."

"Your father ever marry again?"

Gray Feather shook his head. "No. Never had any time for marriage. There was always his business to tend to."

"Maybe it wasn't a matter of time," Kit said, sensing something in his friend's voice.

Gray Feather looked at him. "What else could it have been?"

"Maybe he still thinks of your ma in that special sort of way. Only, his world and hers are too different now. Maybe if someday you were to take her back east . . . ?" Kit left the thought unfinished, allowing Gray Feather to fill in the ending. "Come on, let's get moving. Got us a passel of work yet to do tonight."

They had left the horses saddled and now only had to tighten up the cinches.

"She'd never go," Gray Feather said a few minutes later.

Kit raised a questioning eyebrow, his brain having already gone on to other thoughts.

"Back east, I mean. My mother will never leave the tribe, or the mountains."

Kit swung up onto his saddle. "Never?"

Gray Feather lifted himself lightly onto his stout pony. "Never. It would only confirm her worst fears."

"What might those be?"

Gray Feather was frowning when he looked over. "That the Indian is losing. They can't compete against the white man, but right now most of them don't know that. Cultures are always being displaced, Kit. You know that. Manhead's people lost their lands over fifty years ago. Ours will be the next to go. If my mother ever went back east and saw the technology that's there, it would crush her spirit. I couldn't do that to her. And she's too old to accept change."

Kit turned his horse away, letting the subject drop. But just the same, a thought nagged at him. "Never" was a sweeping word that took in a lot of territory. Like the immense prairies to the east or towering mountain to the west, "never" covered a lot of ground and a lot of possibilities. But the one thing it could *never* completely account for was the changeable nature of men.

Backtracking, Kit felt a little like Daniel must have felt stepping into the lion's den, or like Shadrach, Meshach, and Abednego going into the fiery furnace. But he knew he had to at least make an attempt at taking back their pelts. He and more than two dozen other men had labored all winter for those skins. The men depended on the plews for the money they would bring at rendezvous. They needed that money if they were ever going to outfit themselves for the next season. Few, like Gray Feather, ever saved money from year to year.

Thinking it over, Gray Feather's thrift was an example Kit knew he should be paying more attention to. He remembered their earlier talk; the notion of buying himself a little place in Taos held a particular appeal to him now. He did not want to spend the rest of his life trapping beaver and fighting Indians. And the way silk was replacing the beaver trade on the European markets, there could not be many more good years left for men like himself and Bridger, and Meek, Sublette, and hundreds of others like them.

They dipped down into a wooded ravine and started up the dark side of the next rise, following a game trail. The trail was all but invisible to the men, although the horses seemed to know exactly where to place their next step. Near its crest, Kit and Gray Feather dismounted and went the rest of the way on foot. Working down through the timber, they came to a place where the dark sweep of the valley opened up before their eyes. Just as Gray Feather had predicted, and Kit had somehow known all along, the Blackfeet were camped around the remains of the bonfire the trappers had built hours before. The flames had died back to a small, flickering fire at the edge of a large bank of glowing coals.

"They're all asleep except for those two," Gray Feather whispered, pointing at the remains of the fire where a brave was sitting with a blanket around his shoulders. The Indian had just tossed a couple of sticks onto the faltering flames. His partner was sitting with his back against a rock that helped reflect some of the heat back at them.

Kit's eyes moved from the two drowsy guards to the horses that had been hobbled and turned out to the grass on the other side of the stream. Scattered about lay sleeping forms huddled in their blankets. It was a peaceful setting—that is, if you could ever consider a den of rattlesnakes as a peaceful place to be, he mused.

Kit's main interest, however, was not the guards or the horses, or the sleeping warriors, but the pile of beaver skins stacked neatly off to one side, along with the pack frames that had been removed from the horses before turning them out to pasture.

Kit nudged Gray Feather and pointed. "Thar they are, and thar not being guarded."

"Of course not," Gray Feather said. "No one would be crazy enough to try to steal them from right under their sleeping noses. Nobody but Kit Carson, that is."

Kit only grinned. "Let's give those guards a while. They look to be about ready to fall asleep too."

"Let's hope there isn't a changing of the guards," Gray Feather said.

That would tie a knot in Kit's scheme. For the moment, however, all they could do was wait, and hope the sentries would not be replaced.

The fire burned lower. At one point Kit thought it would flicker out, but then a sleepy guard sat up with a start, stretched, and tossed another stick onto the flames, then leaned back against the rock, drawing his blanket up tight to his chin.

"They're flagging," Gray Feather whispered.

"Not too soon, either. Thar's only another two or three hours of night left. Come on, let's get in a little closer." Moving with the stealth of a panther, Kit started down the steep slope, pausing near the bottom in a clump of juniper along the trail. Gray Feather eased soundlessly beside him.

Kit could not see as far along the valley from here, but he still had a clear view of the two guards near the fire. They hadn't moved in several minutes, and again the flames were burning low.

"This might not be the best time to mention this, Kit, but have you given any thought to how we're going to carry those bundles up here without making enough noise to wake the dead?"

"We aren't going to. We'll take them that way." Kit inclined his head down the valley.

"But that's the way we came."

Kit looked over, hardly able to see his friend's

face in the deep shadows. "If you were Bug's Boys, following a couple men who you gave you the slip, where's the last place you'd look for them?"

The glint of moonlight showed Gray Feather rolling his eyes. "Not again," the Ute said, obviously weary of this new game Kit insisted on playing.

Kit grinned. "Whal, I'll tell you. The last place you'd think of looking for 'em is down your back trail."

Startled, Gray Feather glanced down the valley, the way they had come the day before, and the way the Blackfeet had followed them an hour or so afterward. "You mean you and I are just going to sashay down the same trail we made coming up?"

"Not only will I tell you that, I'll also say that all those tracks that Bug's Boys left behind them will help cover our own as we leave. Now, let's see about moving them plews down the trail and around that bend where them Blackfeet won't be able to see us loading them onto our horses.

Kit left his rifle and made the first run. Fortunately, none of the sleeping Blackfeet had chosen to curl up in their blankets right next to the plews. The nearest was more than twenty feet away. Still, men accustomed to wilderness living never slept very soundly—not if they wanted to see the dawn. A wrong move, a misplaced footstep, a fumble, and Kit would have the whole war party awake in an instant.

The biggest risk came when he left the shadows and crossed a dozen yards of open ground. If the sentries by the fire were still awake, the plan would be over before it started and Kit and Gray Feather would be scrambling to keep their scalps.

But Kit made his way to the pile of beaver skins with no alarm being sounded. The guards were as sound asleep as the rest of the men lying about the ground. He carefully lifted the first heavy bundle and, taking great care to make no sound, backed away toward the brushy growth along the trail where Gray Feather waited for him, his rifle ready just in case.

Kit crept along as if his feet had eyes, carefully testing each step to make certain no brittle twig lay beneath the sole of his moccasin. Back in the shadows, he set the bundle down.

"That wasn't so hard," he whispered. "You get the next one."

Kit held his breath as Gray Feather stole out of cover and sidled up against the pile of plews. Hidden from view in the stack's shadow, Gray Feather listened a moment. He wrapped his arms around the top bundle and, silently turning away, slipped across the ground as noiselessly as Kit had.

Hidden once again, Gray Feather drew in a deep breath. "A teaching job is looking more and more favorable to me all the time, Kit."

"You did just fine."

"With my heart in my throat the whole way."

Kit laughed beneath his breath. "Before we try it again, let's move these two bundles down the trail a piece and stash 'em out of sight of those Injuns, just in case we have to make a quick getaway."

They hauled their prizes around a bend in the trail, hid them in some brush, and went back and performed the ritual all over again. Their luck held out, and inside of an hour they had neatly transferred every bundle out of sight and sound of the Blackfeet, ending with the pack frames, which seemed light as feathers compared to the bundles of beaver pelts they had just carried.

With still an hour or more of darkness ahead of them, Kit and Gray Feather hurried back for the horses and led them to the place where they had hidden the plews. They worked swiftly and expertly, each man having loaded and unloaded animals in just this fashion hundreds of times during the season. With the three extra horses fully loaded, more than five bundles of pelts still had to be left behind. It couldn't be helped, but if the skins managed to escape the notice of the Blackfeet, Kit would be back for them once the danger had passed.

Kit quickly untied the buffalo-hide pads on the horses' hooves. With Gray Feather's help, they coaxed the horses to walk backward down the trail a few hundred yards. Once again they replaced the pads, tightening the thongs that held them in place.

After swinging up onto their saddles, they moved the horses a dozen paces to the left of the trail and started them out of the valley.

Time was still on their side, but with the coming of dawn, it wouldn't be but a few moments after awakening that the Blackfeet would discover the theft that had occurred right in the middle of their sleeping camp.

Kit hoped to be off the trail and well hidden by then. He was grinning as they left the valley behind them. He and Gray Feather had retrieved most of the stolen pelts and had gained a good march on his enemy.

Kit was feeling large and bold, and right pleased with himself. . . .

Chapter Thirteen

"They'll be breathing down our necks as soon as dawn pokes her rosy nose over that ridge," Gray Feather said, scanning the eastern sky, which had begun to grade from black to dark blue.

Kit was searching the trail before them, looking for a place to turn the animals off it without leaving a telltale sign for the Blackfeet to follow. He found what he was looking for a few minutes later in the form of a recent landslide that had swept down the mountainside and into a ravine below. Kit reined to a stop and studied the slide in the growing light. It was probably made a month or two earlier, judging from the sharp edges and still-unsteady nature of the stones. But already a new trail had begun to cut its way across it. Kit noted the tracks left behind when the Blackfeet had crossed this area the day before. A few hundred feet beyond the slide the trail curved sharply, so it was impossible for Kit to see what lay beyond.

"Reckon it's time we give Bug's Boys the slip for good," Kit said, dismounting. They started the animals down the dangerous slope. It was gradual going on either side of the slide, but the point was to leave no tracks. Kit would have liked to have had more light to see by, but that couldn't be helped now. He didn't intend to go far. A few hundred feet was all they needed to go, and Kit wanted to be in a position to see the Blackfeet when they passed by.

At the bottom of the ravine flowed a trickle of water. Kit splashed up this rill until they had left the slide area behind. He turned the animals up the opposite side: At the top they tethered the horses out of sight and moved to a place where the trail they had been following was in plain view. From this vantage point Kit could see the slide and far down both sides of the trail.

Suddenly he thought of something. "I'll be right back."

"Where are you going?"

"Just checking" was all he said. He scrambled down into the ravine again and started up the slide. It had occurred to Kit that the buffalo-hide pads the horses wore worked just fine on flat ground, but on these sharp rocks they could give away the ruse in a minute to a sharp-eyed Blackfoot tracker.

The day was brightening and the stones quickly emerging from night's dark fist. Kit's keen eyes scanned the place where the horses had come down. Then he spied what he feared he might: a clump of buffalo fur clinging to a rock. Kit gathered it up and quickly continued on, snatching the clumps of fur left behind by the pads. He worked all the way back to the top and searched until he was satisfied he'd found them all. He scrambled down again and back to where Gray Feather was waiting.

"What was that all about?"

Kit opened his fingers, showing the Indian the fistful of fur he had collected. "I think I got it all. If Bug's Boys got a glimpse of this, they'd figure out our dodge in two shakes of a lamb's tail.

"I'd have never thought of that."

"Keep your fingers crossed."

Morning stretched out. They waited. Kit's stomach grumbled for lack of food. He and Gray Feather shared the last of their dried venison. The sun reached the ridge and warmed their backs and the ground around them, drawing from it a rich perfume of dried pine needles and last year's aspen leaves. It was beginning to look like the Blackfeet had given up the chase.

Kit could not imagine them accepting the loss of all their pelts without at least giving a cursory search for them. Perhaps his backtracking had worked so well that the Blackfeet had set off in an entirely different direction. Kit almost wished they would show up. At least then he would know where they stood with this war party. If they never did, Kit would always be looking over his shoulder, expecting a surprise attack at any moment.

"You thinking what I'm thinking, Kit?"

"That maybe we got clean away this time?"

"It's beginning to look that way."

Kit frowned. It *was* beginning to look that way, but everything Kit knew about the Blackfeet told him they were not so easily fooled. For perhaps the tenth time that morning, Kit checked the caps on his rifle and pistol. Gray Feather followed suit. Between them they carried six guns—hardly enough to defeat two dozen Blackfeet.

It was beginning to look as if all their preparation was for nothing when—

Kit felt a tug at his sleeve. Gray Feather was pointing.

"Spoke too soon."

It was almost a relief to Kit when he saw the first of the Blackfeet's horses appear far down the right-hand bend in the trail.

"Here they come." His fist tightened around the rifle. "Just took them a little longer than I expected."

"You seem almost pleased."

"I've said it more than once. It's the Injuns I don't see that worry me the most." A tingle of anticipation ran up his spine. Now that they had arrived, Kit fervently hoped they would continue on past the slide area. As they drew nearer, it became plain that the Blackfeet were not scouting a trail. They merely appeared to be returning the way they had come. Perhaps they *had* given up on recovering the pelts and were interested only in returning home to their lodges. This could work out better than Kit had hoped.

"They must have scouted around and figured we'd given them the slip. I think if we sit tight here for a few hours, all our problems will be behind us."

Gray Feather's lips twitched into a brief smile. "Or ahead of us, as the case may be."

As the Blackfeet approached the slide, Kit found that he was holding his breath. But they did not even slow to examine the area, and instead rode right over the rocks and kept on going.

"We did it!" Gray Feather was amazed. He stuck out a hand. Grinning, Kit clasped it, and both men heartily shook. "Remind me to buy you a cigar when we get to the rendezvous."

"Cigar? After last night this child wants a tankard of Bill Sublette's finest sipping whiskey." Kit felt a worrisome weight lifting from his shoulders. The Blackfeet had passed them by, and from the looks of it they were not even searching for tracks. And they had not discovered the five bundles of pelts that Kit had to leave behind, either!

"Then that's what I'll buy you," Gray Feather said, as full of relief as Kit was.

Kit was pleased enough to want to stretch out in the sunshine right there and then and light up a pipe of tobacco and have himself a long, relaxing smoke. And he would have, too, if what he saw next hadn't instantly driven the festivity from him, replacing it with a sudden, cold dread.

Gray Feather's own smile froze when he saw Kit's expression harden and his eyes narrow. "What?" he asked cautiously.

"Damnation! Look at that!"

The Blackfeet were nearing the bend in the trail. From his vantage point, Kit could see what the Indians yet could not. Two hundred yards beyond, coming up the trail, was Petey . . . and in a few minutes both would come face-to-face with each other!

"He's supposed to be back with Manhead!" Gray Feather said.

"Apparently Petey don't listen too well. And now it's gonna cost him."

"He's talking to someone," Gray Feather said, squinting hard to try to bring the distant figure into better focus. "Who could he be talking to? He seems mighty upset over something."

Kit studied the loner and said, "He's talking to that rifle of his again."

"Crazy coot."

"That crazy coot is about to be a dead coot in

another minute. Come on, we got to warn him."

"What about the horses?"

"Let 'em be. They're safe enough here." Kit was already moving. Hunched low, Gray Feather followed after him. The two trappers plunged down into the ravine and scrambled up the other side. Kit was hoping he could catch Petey's attention and flag him off the trail before the Blackfeet saw him, but even as he rushed through the trees, just out of sight of the war party, Kit knew he was not going to make it in time.

Racing low to the ground, Kit batted away the branches and leaves that rose up before him. In a clearing he sped across a covering of kinnikinnick, nearly snagging his foot in the woody, ground-clinging runners. He attempted to keep to thicker timber, avoiding open spaces, but that was not always possible. His path carried him more or less parallel to the war party, and as yet the Indians had not noticed him and Gray Feather. The Blackfeet had not yet turned the bend; both they and Petey were still unaware of each other.

But that was all about to change.

As he dodged low, leaping deadfalls and darting left and right to avoid obstacles in his path, Kit half considered leaving Petey to his fate. It would serve him right. If he had remained with Manhead as Kit had told him to, his life would not be in peril now. And neither would Kit's or Gray Feather's. Kit cursed the man's orneriness. But in spite of his exasperation, he could not let the irascible codger march blindly into the jaws of death without at least trying to help.

A glance showed that Gray Feather was steering a zigzagging course through the forest about a dozen feet to Kit's left. The heavier timber there offered a bit more cover, but it was slowing the Ute too.

The Blackfeet were almost at the bend now. Kit put on a burst of speed, throwing caution to the wind. The Blackfeet were about to know he was there in another moment anyway, and an extra few seconds of warning to Petey might be the edge he needed to dive for cover.

Bursting into the open and leaping atop a rock in plain sight of both the Blackfeet and Petey, Kit waved his rifle high overhead and shouted, "Run for timber, Petey! Bug's Boys up ahead!"

Stunned, Petey stopped and looked all around him, taking a defensive stance, his rifle coming to bear. He cast a worried glance to Kit, then to the side of the trail, and dove for cover as nimbly as if he were twenty years old instead of somewhere north of forty.

Kit dove for the cellar too. At the same time a chorus of war whoops exploded from the throats of two dozen Blackfoot warriors. Half their number spurred their horses and took off down the trail after Petey. The rest reined off the trail and charged into the undergrowth.

In the scramble, Kit lost track of Gray Feather, and Petey had been too far away to know where he had gotten off to anyway. Kit could only hope that the coot had gone to ground and found a hole to crawl into. Kit elbowed behind a boulder where the brush grew thicker, backed in among a bramble of raspberries, and drew a pistol.

The crashing of hooves sounded all around him as horses plunged past. Kit waited, listening, hardly breathing. Now there was a different sound. Some of the Indians had dismounted and were beating the brush for him. The snap of a branch riveted his attention. Someone was just on the other side of the boulder. . . .

Kit's fingers tightened about the pistol. Silently he eased back the heavy hammer. A warrior crept warily into view. His head was turned away as he probed the shadows to the right of him, and he did not immediately see Kit. Kit took the advantage, launching himself at the Indian while at the same time swinging the barrel of the pistol around with all his strength. Its steel barrel slammed against the man's temple, instantly driving him to the ground. The Indian groaned softly, tried to rise. A second blow silenced him.

Looking around, Kit counted; five horsemen had already moved past him. They seemed to not have heard the sound, for their eyes were still turned ahead. Somewhere in that direction Gray Feather was lying low. Kit only hoped his Ute friend had found himself a deep enough hole to curl up in.

Suddenly Kit's neck hairs bristled. He didn't wait to investigate a cause for it but instantly threw himself aside. An arrow whistled past his ear and thunked into a tree two paces ahead. Kit hit the ground rolling and came around to face an Indian diving for him. There was the look of murder in the Blackfoot's face, the glint of steel in his fist. Instinctively, Kit leveled the pistol and squeezed its trigger.

The report echoed throughout the forest, and at once everyone knew exactly where he was. Kit sprang to his feet, dodging trees in his mad flight. An arrow whistled past his head; another skinned the side of his hunting shirt. He heard hoofbeats behind him growing louder. Unlimbering his second pistol, Kit wheeled and fired. The Blackfoot howled and flew off his horse, landing at Kit's feet. The horse plunged on past before Kit could grab a fistful of mane.

Then another pistol cracked. From its direction Kit knew that Gray Feather had been found.

Kit started for his friend, but before he'd gone six paces three Indians suddenly burst through the vegetation to block his way. They came on in single file, one behind the other. The lead man was nocking an arrow as he ran. Kit had only time enough to tilt up his rifle and yank back on the trigger. The big thirty-two-gauge buffalo gun bellowed like thunder, belched smoke and lead, and kicked like a mule in Kit's hand. Ten feet ahead of him the first Indian lurched back as if running into a brick wall. The Indian behind him spun away too and sprawled onto the ground. The half ounce of lead from Kit's rifle had punched a bloody hole through both men's chests. The third Indian, a giant of a man with huge arms and a short, powerful neck, stopped, stunned at the sight of both his comrades falling before the single shot. He recovered in an eyeblink and, yanking a tomahawk from his belt, let loose with a bloodcurdling cry and charged Kit.

Kit reversed the rifle in his hands and drove its curved, steel butt plate at the Indian's face. In spite of his size, the Blackfoot was jackrabbit quick. He dodged left and came in low, swinging out with the short ax. Kit leaped back, unable to retain his hold on his rifle as the steel sliced the buckskin of his hunting shirt. Fast as a rattlesnake strike, the Indian pressed the attack, his tomahawk singing through the air as Kit backpedaled out of its deadly reach.

Another pistol cracked. Gray Feather's second shot. Kit needed to get to his friend's side soon, but at the moment he had a greater problem. He grabbed his own tomahawk from his belt and threw it up in time to block the Blackfoot's downward stroke, a blow that would have cleaved his head if it had landed. Metal rang as the two weapons clashed. Out of the corner of his eye, Kit saw that two more horsemen were bound for the place where the pistol shots had rung out.

Gray Feather needed his help—now!

Chapter Fourteen

"This is a hootin'-an'-a-hollerin' mess we got ourselves into this time!" Petey yelped, holding his hat to his head as he flew through the forest. Kit's warning had given him a brief lead on the Blackfeet, but they were on horseback and he was not. A glance over his shoulder gave Petey a fright. He put on a burst of steam, arms and legs pumping like pistons gone wild.

"Lord Almighty, Betsy! If we ever get out of this mess, I'm walking the straight and narrow. I'm heading back to Bernice! What's that ye say? Ye're right. If we do manage to haul our bacon from this frying pan, it's that coon, Kit Carson, we got to thank."

Petey drew up all of a sudden. "*Kit!* He's got hisself a pack of them savages breathing down his hinder side. That coon needs our help! Now, don't ye argue with me, Betsy! If it warn't for him, we'd be guests of honor at a scalping party right now—

might yet be." Petey spun about, dropping to one knee. He shoved Betsy into his shoulder, drew a bead on the nearest Blackfoot, touched the front trigger of his flintlock Hawken rifle. The rifle sparked and boomed mightily, and the Indian flipped off the horse.

Petey cackled in delight. He shook a defiant fist at the rest of them and dashed off to his left, reloading Betsy on the fly, spilling powder and dropping balls. He finally managed to get the piece loaded and the pan primed. When he wheeled around a second time again, however, he was shocked to discover that the horsemen had disappeared.

"Taken to cover, have ye?" he whispered, hunkering low. His eyes sifted the shadows and shapes in the forest. "Ye red bastards! Whal, two can play this game." Petey had the patience of a saint. He'd wait them out. He hovered in the shadows, his bulging eyes methodically probing the forest. A horse whinnied some distance away. Another pranced into view and trotted riderless back onto the trail.

"Thar a-foot, Betsy. Did ye get a count? . . . Dadburn it, I didn't have me enough time either. . . . Yeah, I'd guess six or eight too."

Another gun shot echoed among the trees. Petey crept from cover and started toward the place where Kit and Gray Feather were battling the Blackfeet.

Twang!

Petey dove to the forest floor. The angry whisper of an arrow buzzed overhead. Petey rolled to his stomach, caught a glimpse of bronze skin in his sights, and fired. Someone yelped. Petey scrambled to his knees and shuffled to cover behind a tree.

"They's all over the place," he panted as his hands

raced for his powder horn and bullet bag. Ramming a ball hard against the charge, he primed the pan with powder from a smaller horn and cautiously pushed an eye around the trunk of the tree. "I know ye're out thar. Show yourselves, ye red devils. I ain't got all day."

Another shot came from up ahead, but this time Petey stayed put, trying to watch everywhere at once.

"Beginning to look like ye an' me, we won't ever get to see that Oreegon country after all, Betsy."

When Kit's first pistol shot had reverberated through the forest, its sound had traveled down the canyon and echoed faintly in the valley below.

At once Joe Meek brought the company of men to a halt and cocked an ear. "Did ya hear that, Gabe?"

"Pistol shot, from the sound of it," Jim Bridger replied, drawing up alongside Meek. He leaned forward in his saddle as his mountain-trained eyes narrowed and scanned far up the trail. "It could be them."

"Has to be them. Couldn't be anyone else!" Meek declared.

Carlos Archuleta said, "What are we waiting for, men? Judging by all these Injun tracks we've been following, if it's Kit, he'll need our help!"

The mountain air was filled with a sudden clatter of rifles as the men checked their weapons. A shout went up from over a hundred throats. Meek put heels to the flanks of his horse and led the charge up the trail.

The faint echo of a second shot told them that the battle was less than a mile ahead and that they did not have a moment to waste.

* * *

Kit slashed and leaped back. The burly Blackfoot expertly deflected the blow, charging in with another barrage that drove Kit up against a tree trunk. With nowhere left to go, Kit's only hope was in finding an opening for his tomahawk while keeping the Indian's own weapon at bay.

The Blackfoot was a big man, with powerful arms that would wear Kit down in another few moments if he didn't do something quickly. As yet this fellow had not been joined by his companions, and that worried Kit. It meant that the bulk of the Blackfeet had descended upon Gray Feather. The thought of his friend's immediate peril sent a shot of renewed vigor to Kit's flagging muscles.

If he couldn't outmuscle this opponent he would have to outthink him. Feigning a dodge to his right, Kit momentarily lowered his guard, giving the Indian a clear opening. As he had hoped, the big warrior took advantage of it, aiming the short ax at Kit's head. Instead of going right, however, Kit dropped immediately to his haunches. The unexpected ploy removed Kit easily from the path of destruction. The tomahawk swung two feet above his head and buried itself into the tree trunk.

Without a break in stride, Kit lunged forward, swinging across. The head of his tomahawk bit deeply into the Indian's side, cleaving between his two lowest ribs. The warrior let out a howl and released his weapon, but immediately he grabbed Kit into his powerful arms. Kit tried to yank his ax free. It had gone deep and was lodged in place. Struggling hand to hand, there was still crushing strength left in the warrior's arms. Kit buried a fist in the washboard stomach, but he was clasped so tightly he could put little strength behind the punch. The giant was squeezing the life from Kit. His ears began to roar. Past the torrent of the rushing blood, Kit heard the report of a rifle—this time from down the trail.

Petey had joined the fray.

It was useless to try to muscle his way out of this fix. The only avenue Kit had open to him was the tomahawk that still clung tenaciously to the muscle and bone in the Indian's side. Bringing down a fist, Kit slammed the tomahawk's head. Its blade bit deeper into the muscle. Again and again Kit pounded the ax into the man's side, until the pain became more than the giant could bear. Dropping Kit, he staggered back, grappling at the tomahawk, attempting to wrench it free.

Kit's lungs burned. Each breath was like taking in red-hot coals. Ignoring the fire, Kit threw a flying kick, landing a heel into the Indian's jaw. His teeth crashed together, and instantly blood gushed from a split lip. The Indian went to his knees. Kit's fist swept up, snapping the man's head back and laying the Indian out cold.

Anchoring a foot into the man's chest, Kit wrenched the tomahawk free and was off and running. He slowed only long enough to grab up his rifle from the forest floor, then turned his steps to Gray Feather's aid.

"Hoss! Duck your head!"

Kit did not have to be warned twice. As he barreled headlong into the ground, an arrow sizzled the air only inches above him. It was followed immediately by the report of Petey's rifle. Up ahead a Blackfoot spun about and disappeared in a clump of juniper. Petey raced up and snagged Kit beneath the arm. "Bug's Boys hot on our asses, hoss! Let's get the hell outta here!"

"Gray Feather needs our help."

"Gray Feather? Whar is the coon?" Petey asked,

breathing hard and scanning the forest for sign of Blackfeet.

"This way!" Kit was running again. His guns were spent and he had no time to tend to them. As he dashed toward the place where he had last heard Gray Feather's pistol bark, he had visions of his friend beneath a horde of vengeful Indians. He pictured Gray Feather fighting to his last breath, then succumbing to the savages' deathblows. He envisioned a Blackfoot warrior even now in the act of lifting his friend's hair. The thought sent shivers down Kit's spine, and he poured on the speed.

Kit spied three of the Indians' horses up ahead. As he strode recklessly nearer, he recalled Gray Feather telling him once that there was no word in the Ute language for good-bye—unlike in English. Kit prayed that he'd reach his friend in time so that *he* did not have to utter that fateful word. . . .

Kit broke out into a clearing. Ahead, all he could see were Blackfeet circled around something. From their center he glimpsed the butt of a rifle swinging out at them.

Gray Feather was still alive!

"Look over here, you red devils!" Kit shouted at them. "This child claims a piece of your mangy hides!"

Two of the Indians stepped aside at Kit's challenge. Past them Kit had a clearer view of the battle beyond. Gray Feather was still alive but flagging. He had been backed against a tree, and with blood streaming down the side of his face he wielded his rifle like a club in a last-ditch effort to keep the Blackfeet back. But he was losing ground, only just managing to keep the Indians at bay. It appeared as though Bug's Boys were holding back on purpose, taunting the man. They knew the Ute was defeated already. They were only toying with him, wearing him down, about ready to issue the final deathblow. Even as Kit sped through the forest, two of the warriors nocked arrows in their gut-string bows and began to draw them back.

Kit cocked back an arm, aiming his tomahawk. It was a desperate act of a desperate man, since the distance was yet too great for Kit to reach them, or to fling the ax with any accuracy. But even if he could have reached Gray Feather's side, Fate seemed to have different plans, and she stepped in and barred his way, laughing at the puny efforts of a mere mortal man. Fate, in the shape of a Black-foot warrior, suddenly leaped in Kit's path and lurched forward with his five-foot-long war lance.

Kit wrenched his body sideways. The iron-pointed spear skimmed past him. Kit hacked down with the tomahawk, knocking the lance aside. As if performing a carefully choreographed dance routine, Kit pirouetted around on one foot, swinging his ax into the attacker's shoulder, cracking through his collarbone. With a howl of agony the Indian went down, but Kit did not move fast enough and he tripped over the falling man, sprawling headfirst.

Stunned, Kit tried to raise himself. The fall had knocked the breath from him, and it took a supreme effort just to draw in a breath. Kit was vaguely aware of someone trying to help him up. But his view was riveted ahead, locked in horror as he watched the two bowmen take aim at Gray Feather . . . and there was not a thing Kit could do now to save his friend.

Then Fate, being the fickle creature she is, changed her mind. As if materializing out of nothingness, Fate was suddenly in the Indians' midst—Fate in the shape of nearly a thousand pounds of violent, slashing death and destruction.

"Gol-dang!" Stunned awe was in Petey's voice. He was beside Kit, trying to drag the mountain man to his feet.

"It's Ebenezer!" Kit said.

The giant bear had reared up somewhere behind the Blackfeet encircling Gray Feather. Over nine feet tall and venting all the anger and hatred the huge grizzly harbored toward these Indians, he lashed out with the great, glistening sickles at the end of his paws.

The first swipe scattered Indians as if they had been a row of ninepins. The air shook with Ebenezer's savage roar. With an odd mix of horror and fascination, Kit watched the massive jaws clamp down on the shoulder of one man. Muscles rippled beneath the silver-gray coat of fur, the beast's head arched back, and the fellow flew a dozen feet into the trunk of a tree.

As if understanding Gray Feather's peril, Ebenezer placed his giant body between the Ute and the pressing horde of Blackfeet. One of the bowmen swiveled and let loose a shaft. The arrow impaled the bear in the left shoulder. Its sting only intensified the grizzly's rage. Wheeling, a gigantic paw swept out, gleaming claws ripping open stomach muscle as if it were no more substantial than the flimsy web a spider spins between two trembling branches.

Another arrow flew. Ebenezer roared and turned. Two more Blackfeet fell beneath the lashing paws and snapping teeth. Kit saw a third arrow slam into the bear.

"Got to give him a hand," Kit said, pushing himself to his knees and then to his feet. Drawing his butcher knife in one hand and his tomahawk in the other, he rushed into the fray. His tomahawk flashed in a beam of sunlight through the tree cover. An Indian yelped and collapsed. Petey swung his rifle, cracking open one skull and then another. Kit lost track of all that was happening around him, his whole world suddenly compressed down to the knife and ax in his fist, and the nine or ten Blackfeet still standing.

Chapter Fifteen

The tide of the battle turned. The Indians had seen something terrifying in the arrival of Ebenezer. Perhaps, Kit thought, they beheld an evil omen in this majestic grizzly. Any bear who would fight on the side of the trappers was certainly a beast not from this world. Perhaps the netherworld had opened up in their land and from it had issued this beast—this tormentor of the Blackfeet, sent especially to vex them. After all, was it not this very same bear who had terrorized their campsite only days before?

Whatever their thoughts, they suddenly retreated en masse, scrambling for their horses, dragging their wounded and dying comrades with them.

The Blackfeet were on the run, but Kit was too weary to take the advantage. He leaned against a tree, breathing hard. Gray Feather had slumped to his knees, supported only by the grip he had retained around the barrel of his rifle.

"The critters are hightailing it," Petey gasped, drawing in huge gulps of air.

The ground was littered with bodies, but miraculously, Kit, Gray Feather, and Petey were not among them. . . .

"Ebenezer!" Kit said suddenly, looking around for the bear. He saw the bear stagger away, then stumble and go to his knees.

"No!" Petey cried, dropping his rifle and running to the fallen beast.

Kit gave Gray Feather a hand up. "You hurt bad?"

Gray Feather wiped the blood from his head and pressed a hand to a gash there. "Got too near to one of their tomahawks," he said. "I think I'll be all right."

Just then they heard the pounding of hooves coming up the trail. In a moment the great company of mountain men rode into view. Coming upon the scene, Kit saw Meek give an order and twenty men broke formation and went charging off after the fleeing Blackfeet.

Kit gave a whistle and waved, catching their attention. Meek, Bridger, and what looked to Kit to be most of an army of trappers turned their horses into the forest.

"Good Gawd!" Meek declared, staring at the bodies strewn about. He looked at Kit and Gray Feather, assured himself that neither man was badly wounded, and said, "Doggone it, Kit, I told you to leave some for me. Here you went and punished them all by yourself!"

"You're about five minutes late, Joe," Kit said, reveling in their miraculous survival and the prospect once again of a future. But now his concern was focused on the bear, as ridiculous as that might have seemed to him. "We have Ebenezer to thank for our scalps still being attached." Kit and Gray Feather went to the bear.

"He's bad hurt," Petey said with a catch in his voice. He had the grizzly's broad head upon his legs, his fingers clutching the coarse fur at the bear's neck.

Ebenezer had taken three arrows—arrows that would have been meant for Gray Feather had not the bear shown up. Two of the wounds were minor, but the third arrow had buried itself deep in the bear's back, behind the shoulder and below the hump—a vulnerable place for a grizzly.

The trappers held back, their natural suspicion of bears making them cautious. But Meek and Bridger came closer. As they did, Ebenezer grew agitated and began to toss his head.

"Ye're making him nervous," Petey barked.

Bridger and Meek retreated. Ebenezer relaxed, however, when Gray Feather and Kit approached.

"This doesn't look good, Kit," Gray Feather said.

"Appears Ebenezer has come to the end of his trail," Kit allowed with a heavy sadness pressing down his spirits.

"Maybe we can cut them out?" Petey implored.

Gray Feather was frowning. "We ought to at least try to do something."

Kit shook his head. "Don't see how I can do it. That one in the back, it's gonna take more of a surgeon than I am. It's most likely lodged near his heart."

"A surgeon?" Gray Feather glanced at the army of mountain men who were waiting some distance away, watching with open curiosity. "Kit, I thought I saw Doc Whitman among them." He was still scanning the faces.

"Whitman?" Kit's gaze swept around the clearing. Whitman was hunkered over the body of one of the Blackfeet.

"Think he'll try?" Petey asked.

Kit grimaced. "Likely to think we're crazy for asking, but it's worth a try, I reckon." Kit went to where the doctor was tending the fallen Indian. As he did, Gray Feather hurried back to his horse for the volume of the collected works of Shakespeare that he always carried with him in his saddlebags.

"You want me to do *what*?" Whitman declared.

"Least you can have a look at him," Kit pressed.

The doctor frowned and said, "I've never heard of such a thing," but he came back with Kit anyway. Perhaps it was curiosity more than anything else that convinced him to give it a try—once Kit assured him that Ebenezer was a friendly sort of bear, and quite peaceable when Gray Feather was reading to him.

With a deft surgeon's hand, Dr. Whitman used a shiny surgical knife to cut deep into Antoine Menard's back. The mountain man was in a bad way. For the last few days Manhead had been keeping him alive with thin soups of rabbit meat and wild roots, forcing the liquid down the sometimes delirious man's throat.

It was only this morning that Menard had passed out and had not regained consciousness. Even in his unconscious state, Manhead had patiently kept nourishment flowing into the man's feverish body. And a few hours after that, Kit, Bridger, and the rest of the trappers arrived. Petey had been a big help in finding the location. Without him, the mountaineers might have hunted for days before discovering the trail into the hideout.

Gray Feather had remained behind with twenty men to show them the way back to where the rest of their pelts had been hidden. Kit expected the Ute along in a day or two. The mountain men had left a train wide enough for a greenhorn to follow. There was not concern about Indians. Now that the trappers were over a hundred men strong, no tribe would dare to attack them.

Kit and Bridger were hunkered around a fire. Kit was relating the events of the past week when Doc Whitman came over and showed him four inches of arrow, including an iron head.

"I'm getting quite a collection of these," he said. He nodded at the coffeepot on a rock, perched above a bank of coals. "I could sure use some of that."

Kit poured him a cup. "Is he gonna make it, Doc?"

Whitman gave an indefinite shake of his head. "I did all I could. The lung will heal in time—that is, if he lives long enough. But an infection has set in. I haven't got any medicine to treat that."

"The Indians have remedies," Bridger said. "Things white doctors have never heard of."

"Yes, I know. Manhead and a few of the other Delawares have offered to help. They are seeing to it now. But I'm afraid in the end it is up to Menard's will to live, and the hand of God. Lord knows, I did all that I can for him."

"A man can only do what he's able to," Kit allowed.

"Amen to that," Whitman agreed.

"Me and some of the boys will stay here as long as we have to. You and the Doc and the others can start back to Horse Creek whenever you want to, Gabe."

Bridger shook his head, frowning into his coffee cup. "We'll all stay for a few days, Kit. After all, still a passel of Blackfeet and Crows about. Wouldn't want no more misery to befall you and the others. I think every child here will agree with me on that."

Kit looked over at Whitman. "How was Overmier doing when you left him back at the rend'vous?"

"He appeared as if he was going to recover. You did a passable job of cutting those arrows out of him, Kit, though I can't say as much for your stitchery. Overmier will be carrying some right handsome scars for the rest of his days."

Kit grinned halfheartedly. He was exhausted. All he wanted to do was curl up in his blanket and sleep for a week straight.

And that is almost exactly what he did.

One week later the company of men were on the move again. Menard, through the hand of Providence, with a little help from Whitman's surgical knives and the Delawares' knowledge of herbs and teas, was on the mend. The fever had broken, and although his breathing was still labored, he could draw in enough air to turn the air blue with his cursing the bumpy ride he was taking on the travois.

"Tell me again about Oreegon," Petey asked Meek a few days later as Meek and Kit rode side by side behind the travois. The land of spouting fountains, boiling mud, and marauding Blackfeet was far behind them. Up ahead lay Horse Creek.

"It rains pretty near every day," Meek declared. "And it's got forest so green that the very sight of them is enough to blind some weaker men. The trees drip water constantly, and the ground is carpeted with plants the likes of which you've never seen before, Petey. And it's still wide open for the taking."

Petey grinned. "Wide open. I like the sound of that. These here Rocky Mountains are getting a bit too crowded for a coon like us, ain't that right, Betsy?"

Just then a band of half-naked men on horseback appeared along the brow of a ridge. One of them raised a feathered war lance above his head and gave a bloodcurdling cry. In an instant the warriors were plunging down the long slope, whooping like a war party of Comanches. It was trappers coming to greet them and escort them into the rendezvous. Waving bows over their heads, their faces painted in crimson streaks, they looked every bit the wild Indians they were pretending to be.

The mountaineers cheered at their sight, spurred their horses, and dashed forward to meet them. A smile spread Kit's bewhiskered cheeks. The rendezvous had started! It would be a glorious three weeks, and Kit intended to make the most of it.

Petey had reined to a stop, wearing a worried look.

"What's the matter?" Kit asked, pulling up alongside the loner.

"How many men you say are to be here, hoss?" he asked worriedly.

"Sometimes three hundred, including the friendly tribes."

"Three hundred. Hmm, that's a bunch. More than a whole settlement's worth."

"Getting ice in your moccasins?"

Petey stiffened in the saddle. "Nothing scares old Petey Pauly."

"Not even a Blackfoot war party?"

" 'Specially not that," Petey shot back.

"Then you should be right comfortable among your own kind."

"I am," he replied defensively.

"Whal, what are you waiting for? Thar's your own kind." Kit indicated the whooping mountain men galloping down to welcome them into camp.

"Reckon I need to wait here just a little while, hoss." Petey looked at him. "Shoot, Ebenezer is back thar somewhere. He ain't moving so sprightly these days, ye know. I'll just wait for him to catch up."

Kit understood Petey's real concern. After all these years alone with only his rifle and Ebenezer for company, the thought of so many people all in one place was a little frightening.

Kit was still worried how the bear would be received at the rendezvous, but he'd been delighted that the animal had come through Whitman's surgery and, like Menard, was on the mend.

There was no accounting for it, but Kit had become attached to that grizzly bear. It was crazy, he knew, but stranger things have been known to happen.

Kit left Petey waiting there with his excuse . . . and his pride intact, and rode ahead to join the festivities waiting just over the next hill.